An
Officer
and a Lady

and Other Stories

Other Rex Stout books available from Carroll & Graf

AN
OFFICER
AND A LADY

and Other Stories

Rex Stout

CARROLL & GRAF PUBLISHERS, INC.
NEW YORK

First Carroll & Graf edition 2000

Carroll & Graf Publishers, Inc.
A Division of Avalon Publishing Group
19 West 21st Street
New York, NY 10010-6805

Library of Congress Cataloging-in-Publication Data is available.
ISBN: 0-7867-0764-X

Manufactured in the United States of America

CONTENTS

An Officer and
a Lady

🎼

Bill Farden had had his eye on the big brick house on the corner for some time.

He had worked one in that block—the white frame with the latticed porch farther down toward Madison Street—during the early part of March, and had got rather a nice bag. Then, warned off by the scare and hullabaloo that followed, he had fought shy of that part of town for a full month, confining his operations to one or two minor hauls in the Parkdale section. He figured that by now things would have calmed down sufficiently in this neighborhood to permit a quiet hour's work without undue danger.

It was a dark night, or would have been but for the street lamp on the corner. That mattered little, since the right side of the house was in deep shadow anyway. By an oversight I have neglected to place the scene of the story in the vicinity of a clock tower, so Bill Farden was obliged to take out his watch and look at it in order to call attention to the fact that it was an hour past midnight.

He nodded his head with satisfaction, then advanced

across the lawn to that side of the house left in deep shadow.

Two large windows loomed up side by side, then a wide expanse of brick, then two more. After a leisurely examination he chose the second of the first pair. A ray from his electric flash showed the old-fashioned catch snapped to.

Grinning professionally, he took a thin shining instrument from his pocket, climbed noiselessly onto the ledge and inserted the steel blade in the slit. A quick jerk, a sharp snap, and he leaped down again. He cocked his ear.

No sound.

The window slid smoothly upward to his push, and the next instant his deft accustomed hand had noiselessly raised the inner shade. Again he lifted himself onto the ledge, and this time across it, too. He was inside the house.

He stood for a time absolutely motionless, listening. The faintest of scratching noises came from the right.

"Bird," Bill observed mentally, and his experienced ear was corroborated a moment later when the light of his electric flash revealed a canary blinking through the bars of its cage.

There was no other sound, and he let the cone of light travel boldly about the apartment. It was a well-furnished library and music room, with a large shining table, shelves of books along the walls, a grand piano at one end, and several comfortable chairs. Bill grunted and moved toward a door at the farther corner.

He passed through, and a glance showed him the dining room. Stepping noiselessly to the windows to make sure that the shades were drawn tight, he then switched on the electric chandelier. There was promise in the array of china and cut glass spread over the buffet and sideboard, and with an expectant gleam in his eye he sprang to open the heavy drawers.

The first held linen; he didn't bother to close it again.

The second was full of silver, dozens, scores of pieces of old family silver. In a trice Bill flew to the ledge of the window by which he had entered and was back again with a suitcase in his hand.

When the silver, wrapped in napkins, was safely in the suitcase, Bill straightened and glanced sharply around. Should he leave at once with this rare booty so easily gathered? He shook his head with decision and returned to place the suitcase on the window ledge in the library; then he came back, switched off the light in the dining room, and entered the kitchen.

By unerring instinct he stepped to the refrigerator. A flash of his pocket-lamp, and he gave a satisfied grunt. He turned on the light. From the recesses of the ice-box he brought forth a dish of peas, some sliced beef, half a chicken, some cold potatoes, and part of a strawberry shortcake. In a drawer in the kitchen cabinet he found a knife and fork and some spoons.

From a common-sense viewpoint the performance was idiotic. Having broken into an inhabited house in the dead of night, rifled the silver drawer and deposited the loot on the window sill, I for one would not be guilty of the artistic crime of tacking on an anticlimax by returning to the kitchen to rob the refrigerator and grossly stuff myself.

But Bill Farden was an old and experienced hand, thoroughly versed in the best burglar tradition. Also, perhaps he was hungry. He ate as one who respects food but has no time for formalities.

He had finished the meat and vegetables and was beginning on the shortcake, when all of a sudden he sprang noiselessly from his chair to the electric button on the wall. A tiny click and the room was in darkness. He crouched low against the wall, while the footsteps that had startled him from above became louder as they began to descend the back stairs.

There might still be a chance to make the door into the dining room, but he decided against it. Scarcely breathing, he pulled himself together and waited. The footsteps became louder still; they halted, and he heard a hand fumbling at the knob of the stairway door. The noise of the opening door followed.

Bill's mind was working like lightning. Probably someone had been awake and seen the light from a slit through the window shade. Man or woman? He would soon know.

The footsteps sounded on the floor, advancing, and his eyes, accustomed to the darkness, caught a dim outline. Noiselessly his hand sought the side pocket of his coat and fumbled there. The figure approached; it was now quite close, so close that all Bill had to do was rise swiftly to his feet and close his fingers in their viselike grip.

A curious penetrating odor filled the air and a sputtering, muffled cry came from the intruder. A short, sharp struggle, and the form sank limply to the floor. Kneeling down, Bill pressed the damp sponge a little longer against the nostrils and mouth until the body had quite relaxed, then returned the sponge to the pocket that held the chloroform tube.

He switched on the light and surveyed his prostrate anesthetized victim. It was a powerful-looking woman in a blue flannel nightgown; feet large and red, face coarse in feature and of contour Scandinavian; probably the cook. Bill wasted little thought on her. The point was that his blood was up now. He had had the taste of danger and his eyes gleamed. He shot a glance at the open stairway door.

A moment later his shoes were off, strung from his belt by their laces, and he was on his way up—silently, warily. The eleventh step creaked a little and he stopped short.

Two minutes and no sound.

He went on to the top of the stairs and halted there, standing a while to listen before risking his electric flash. Its rays showed him a long wide hall with two doors on one side and three on the other, all closed, so he moved noiselessly on to the farther end, the front of the house, listened a moment at the crack of a door and then cautiously turned the knob and entered, leaving the door open behind him.

His ear told him instantly that he was not alone; the room was occupied; he heard someone breathing. His nerves were drawn tight now, his whole body alert and quivering with the pleasurable excitement of it, like a thoroughbred at the barrier.

A faint reflection of light from the street lamp came in through the window, just enough to make out the dim forms of furniture and the vague lumpy outline under the covers on the bed. He heard a watch ticking; it became less audible when he moved swiftly to the dressing table and transferred the timepiece to his own pocket. He turned as by instinct toward the door of the closet, but halted sharply halfway across the room.

There was something queer about that breathing. He listened tensely. Most irregular. Surely not the respiration of a sleeper—and he was an expert on the subject. Suspicious, to say the least.

Like a flash he was at the bedside, and his sharp gaze detected a shuddering movement all over the form that lay there under the sheets. His hand flew to the side pocket of his coat, then he remembered that the chloroform tube was empty. In a fit of rashness he pressed the button of his pocket-flash, and there on the pillow, in the center of the bright electric ray that shot forth, he saw the face of a man with mouth wide open and eyes staring in abject terror—a man wide awake and petrified with fear.

Bill had seen such countenances before, and experience had taught him to waste no time in taking advantage of the wide-open mouth. So, moving with swift sureness, he filled that gaping aperture with the corner of a sheet, stuffing it in with conscientious thoroughness. Then, while the man made feeble attempts to get loose, which Bill impatiently ignored, he tied his hands and feet and made the gag secure.

Gurglings barely audible came from the victim's nose; our hero made a threatening gesture, and they ceased. He proceeded calmly and methodically to rifle the room and closet. When he finished ten minutes later, he had deposited in various places about his person two silver cigarette cases, three scarf pins, five rings, a jeweled photograph frame, and ninety-four dollars in cash.

He looked to see that his captive was securely tied, scowled ferociously into his face, tiptoed out of the room and closed the door behind him. He had been in the house not more than thirty minutes, and already two of the enemy had been rendered *hors de combat*, a bag of booty was waiting for him below, his stomach was full, and his clothing was loaded with money and jewelry. His chest swelled with pardonable pride. On with the dance!

Inflated and emboldened by success, he flashed his light impudently up and down the hall, finally deciding on the next door to the right on the opposite side. He advanced, noiselessly turned the knob and entered. The light from the street lamp did not enter on this side, and the room was pitch dark.

For a moment he thought it unoccupied, then the sound of faint breathing came to his ear—quite faint and regular. He took a step toward the bed, then, magnificently scorning danger, turned to the wall near the door and felt for the electric button. He pushed; a click, and the room was flooded with light.

On the instant Bill sprang toward the bed, to forestall any outcry of alarm from its occupant. But he halted three paces away, with his arms half outstretched, at the sight that met his gaze.

There, under the silken coverlet, in the glare from the chandelier, he saw a sleeping child.

It was a girl of eight or nine years; her little white arm was curved under her head, and her soft brown hair spread in glorious curled confusion over the pillow. Her breast moved regularly up and down with her gentle breathing, and her sweet red lips were opened a little by the smile of a dream.

Bill stood still and gazed at her. He felt all of a sudden big and dirty and burly and clumsy and entirely out of place, and turning slowly to glance about the room, he saw that it was well suited to its occupant.

There was a small dressing table, a chest of drawers, a writing desk, and two or three chairs, all in dainty pink with delicately figured covers. On one corner of the desk stood a silver telephone instrument. The wall was pure white, with pink flowers and animals scattered in profusion along the border. A low wide bookcase, with full shelves, stood at one end. A pair of little white shoes were in the middle of the floor; on a chair nearby were the stockings and other garments.

Bill looked at them, and at the beautiful sleeping child, and at the child's beautiful room, and he felt something rise in his chest. Slowly his hand went to his head, and off came his cap.

"My little girl would have a place like this," he muttered half-aloud.

The fact that Bill had no little girl or big one either, that he was indeed quite unmarried, is no reason to suspect the sincerity of his emotion. Some fathers might argue that it is in fact a reason to believe in it; but we are interested only in what actually happened. Undoubtedly what Bill meant was this, that if he had had a little girl of his own he would have wanted for her such a room as this one.

He moved close to the bed and stood there looking down at its occupant. What he was thinking was that he had never before realized that a creature could be so utterly helpless without thereby incurring the contempt of a strong man. There was something strangely stirring in the thought. Perhaps after all physical force was not the only power worth having. Here was this little child lying there utterly helpless before him—utterly helpless, and yet in fact far more secure from injury at his hands than a powerful man would have been.

No, force was not made to be used against helpless beings like her. What would he do if she should awake and cry out? He would talk to her and quiet her. According to the best burglar tradition, it would even be allowable to take her on his knee, and if a tear or so appeared in his eye it would be nothing to be ashamed of.

But what if she would not be quieted? What if in her fright she should persist in spreading the alarm? Force, then? No. In that case he would simply beat it. He would drop a kiss on her soft brown hair and make his escape. He did, in fact, bend over the pillow and deposit an extremely clumsy kiss on a lock of her hair, probably in order to have that much done and over with.

He turned away, for he felt one of the tears already halfway to his eye. A shiny something on the dressing table caught his attention and he moved across to inspect it. It was a tiny gold wristwatch with an enameled rim. He picked it up and looked at the name of the maker, and his eyes widened with respect.

Expensive trinket, that. Absurd to trust a child with it. No doubt she was very proud of the thing. He put it down again, spared even the impulse to put it in his pocket. He knew it would be useless to debate the matter with himself. What burglar would take anything from a sweet helpless child like—

"Hands up!"

The words came from behind him. They were uttered in a thin treble voice, as crisp and commanding as the snap of a whip. Bill wheeled like lightning and stood petrified.

The sweet helpless child was sitting up straight in bed, and in her extended hand was a mean-looking little revolver, with the muzzle directed unerringly one inch above the apex of Bill's heart.

"Lord above us!" ejaculated our hero, as his jaw dropped open in astonishment.

There was a short silence. The burglar's attitude of stupefaction became less pronounced, and his jaw came up again to take part in an amused grin as he relaxed, but the steady brown eyes facing him were unwavering in their direct and businesslike gaze.

"I would advise you to put your hands up before I count ten," said the sweet, helpless child calmly. "One, two, three—"

"Really, now," Bill put in hastily, "I wouldn't advise you to shoot, little girl. You might scare someone. I won't hurt you."

"I don't shoot to scare people. I see you don't take me seriously. It may interest you to know that yesterday at the gallery at Miss Vanderhoof's Academy I got nine straight centers from the hip. I am much better with the eye. I am Major Wentworth of Squadron A of the Girls' Military Auxiliary, and I am the crack shot of our regiment. Four, five, six—"

Bill was speechless. He calculated the distance to the bed. Easily ten feet. That revolver barrel was certainly aimed level. Nine straight centers from the hip, and much better with the eye. Coldish business. He hesitated. The brown eyes held his steadily.

"Seven, eight, nine—"

His keen eye saw the muscles of the little wrist begin to tighten. Up went his hands above his head.

"That's better," said the sweet, helpless child approvingly. "I would have pulled the trigger in another half second. I had decided to get you in the right shoulder. Now turn your back, please, but keep your hands up."

Bill did so. Almost immediately came the command to turn about again. She had clambered out of bed and stood there on the rug with her pink nightgown trailing about her feet and her soft brown hair tumbling over her shoulders. She looked more tiny than ever. But the muzzle of the revolver wavered not a fraction of an inch as she stepped sidewise to the wall and pressed her finger against a button there. Nothing was said while she repeated the operation three times. More silence.

"Look here, little girl," Bill began earnestly, "there's no use gettin' your arm all tired with that toy gun. I ain't going to hurt you."

"You may call me Major Wentworth," was all the reply he got.

"All right, Major. But come, what's the use—"

"Stop! If you move again like that I'll shoot. I wonder what's the matter with Hilda. She sleeps very lightly." This last to herself.

Bill looked interested.

"Is Hilda a big sort of a woman in a blue nightgown?"

"Yes. Have you seen her?" The brown eyes filled with sudden alarm. "Oh! Where is she? Is she hurt?"

"Nope." Bill chuckled. "Kitchen floor. Chloroform. I was eatin' strawberry shortcake when she come in."

The major frowned.

"I suppose I must call my father. I hate to disturb him—"

"He's incapable, too," announced Bill with another chuckle. "Tied up with sheets and things. You see, Major, we're all alone. Tell you what I'll do. There's a suitcase full of silver down on the library windowsill. I'll agree to leave it there—"

"You certainly will," the major nodded. "And you'll leave the other things too. I see them in your pockets. Since my father is tied up I suppose I must call the police myself."

She began to move sidewise toward the silver telephone on the desk, keeping the revolver pointed at Bill's breast.

I transcribe Bill's thought: The little devil was actually going to call the police! Action must come now if at all, and quickly. He dismissed the idea of a dash for freedom; she would certainly pull the trigger, and she had a firm eye and hand. Bill summoned all his wit.

"My little girl's mama is dead, too," he blurted out suddenly.

The major, with her hand outstretched for the telephone, stopped to look at him.

"My mother isn't dead," she observed sharply. "She's gone to the country."

"You don't say so!" Bill's voice was positively explosive with enthusiastic interest. "Why didn't you go along, Major, if I may ask?"

"I am too busy with the Auxiliary. We are pushing the campaign for preparedness." She added politely: "You say your wife is dead?"

Bill nodded mournfully.

"Been dead three years. Got sick and wasted away and died. Broke my little girl's heart, and mine, too."

A suggestion of sympathy appeared in the major's eyes as she inquired:

"What is your little girl's name?"

"Her name?" Bill floundered in his stupidity. "Oh, her name. Why, of course her name's Hilda."

"Indeed!" The major looked interested. "The same as Cook. How funny! How old is she?"

"Sixteen," said Bill rather desperately.

"Oh, she's a big girl, then! I suppose she goes to school?"

Bill nodded.

"Which one?"

It was a mean question. In Bill's mind school was simply school. He tried to think of a word that would sound like the name of one, but nothing came.

"Day school," he said at last, and then added hastily, "that is, she moves around, you know. Going up all the time. She's a smart girl." His tone was triumphant.

Then, fearing that another question might finish him, he continued slowly:

"You might as well go on and call the cops—the police, I suppose. Of course, Hilda's at home hungry, but that don't matter to you. She'll starve to death. I didn't tell you she's sick. She's sick all the time—something wrong with her. I was just walkin' past here and thought I might find something for her to eat, and I was lookin' around—"

"You ate the strawberry shortcake yourself," put in the major keenly.

"The doctor won't let Hilda have cake," Bill retorted. "And I was hungry myself. I suppose it's no crime to be hungry—"

"You took the silver and other things."

"I know." Bill's head drooped dejectedly. "I'm a bad man, I guess. I wanted to buy nice things for Hilda. She hasn't had a doll for over ten years. She never has much to eat. If I'm arrested I suppose she'll starve to death."

The sympathy in the major's eyes deepened. "I don't want to cause unnecessary suffering," she declared. "I feel strongly for the lower classes. And Miss Vanderhoof says that our penal system is disgraceful. I suppose little would be gained by sending you to prison."

"It's an awful place," Bill declared feelingly.

"You have been there?"

"Off and on."

"You see! It has done you no good. No, I might as well let you go. Turn your back."

Bill stared.

The major stamped her little bare foot.

"Turn your back, I say! That's right. I do wish you wouldn't make me repeat things. Walk forward near the dressing table. No, at the side. So. Now empty your pockets and turn them inside out. All of them. Put the things on the dressing table. Keep your back turned, or—as you would say in your vulgar parlance—I'll blow your block off."

Bill obeyed. He could feel the muzzle of the revolver pointed directly at the back of his head, and he obeyed. He lost no time about it either, for the anesthetized Hilda would be coming to soon.

Methodically and thoroughly the pockets were emptied and their contents deposited on the dressing table: a gentleman's watch, two silver cigarette cases, three scarf pins, five rings, a jeweled photograph frame, and ninety-four dollars in cash. The articles that were obviously Bill's own she instructed him to return to the pockets. He did so.

"There!" said the major briskly when he had finished. "You may turn now. That's all, I think. Kindly close the front door as you go out. I'll attend to the suitcase on the windowsill after you're gone. I wouldn't advise you to try any tricks on me. I've never got a man on the run, but I'd love to have a crack at one. That's all."

Bill hesitated. His eye was on the neat roll of bills reposing beside him on the dressing table. It traveled from that to the gold wristwatch he would not take because it belonged to the sweet, helpless child. Would he take it now if he had a chance? Would he!

The major's voice came:

"Go, please. I'm sleepy, and you've given me a lot of trouble. I shall have to revive Hilda, if it is possible. I have doubts on the subject. She refuses to keep herself in condition. She eats too much, she will not take a cold bath, she won't train properly, she is sixty-eight pounds overweight, and she sleeps with her mouth open. But she's a good cook—"

"She is that," Bill put in feelingly, with his memory on the shortcake.

"—and I trust she has not expired. There is my father, too. To put it mildly, he is a weakling. His lack of wind is deplorable. He sits down immediately after eating. It is only three miles to his law office, and he rides. He plays golf and calls it exercise. If you have gagged him scientifically he may have ceased breathing by now.

"In one way it would be nothing to grieve over, but he is my father after all, and the filial instinct impels me to his assistance against my better judgment. You do not seem to be in good condition yourself. I doubt if you know how to breathe properly, and it is evident that you do not train systematically. There are books on the subject in the public library; I would advise you to get one. You may give my name as a reference. Now go."

Bill went. The door of the room was open. He started toward the back stairs, but the major halted him abruptly and made him right about; she had switched on the lights in the hall. Down the wide front staircase he tramped, and from behind came the major's voice:

"Keep your mouth closed. Head up! Arms at your side. Breathe through your nose. Chest out forward! Hep, hep, hep—the door swings in. Leave it open. Lift your foot and come down on the heel. Turn the corner sharply. Head up!"

She stood in the doorway as he marched across the porch, down the steps, and along the gravel path to the sidewalk. A turn to the right, and thirty paces took him to the street corner. Still the major's voice sounded from the doorway:

"Hep, hep, hep—lift your feet higher—breathe through your nose—hep, hep, hep—"

And as he reached the street corner the command came sharply:

"Halt! About face! Salute!"

A glance over his shoulder showed him her nightgown framed in the doorway. There were trees in between. Bill halted, but he did not about face and he did not salute. It was too much. Instead, after a second's hesitation, he bounded all at once into the street and across it, and was off like a shot. And as he ran he replied to her command to salute by calling back over his shoulder, as man to man:

"Go to hell!"

EXCESS BAGGAGE

Napoleon may have been imprisoned on an island; Milton may have written "Paradise Lost;" Carrie Nation may have smashed a joint; and Hannibal may have crossed the Alps. But I don't believe it. I believe nothing. When a man's own wife, the woman whom he loves above all the world, is convinced—but listen to my tale and you'll know what I mean.

Since I intend to tell the truth, the whole truth and the rest of it, I may as well admit that before I was married I made no claims to the white badge of purity. At the time I started to grow my first mustache I was a traveling salesman, and I've been one ever since. I remember an old refrain that ended something like this:

> Sailors have sweethearts in every port,
> And drummers in every town.

Perhaps it's a little too flattering; a knight of the road may be attractive and insinuating, but he isn't irresistible. And

besides, there are some towns where a man wouldn't keep
a dog—much less a sweetheart. But the author had the
right idea, generally speaking.

For about twelve years I did all in my power to make
the words of that song ring true; and even yet it puffs me
up a little to remember that for eight of them I was the
champion S.S. of the river route on up as far as St. Albans,
Vt. S.S. means Secret Sorrow. No woman is ever happy
without one. Only if you ever decide to enter the profession, take it from me that it's harder than it looks. It's
easy enough to show a girl a good time; too often it's still
easier to persuade her to do things she shouldn't do. But
you have to have a real knack and lots of practice to be
a genuine Secret Sorrow. Besides, you are continually in
danger of becoming an active member of another organization not quite so popular. In fact, they're so near alike
that it takes an expert to tell them apart—even the names
are similar. Many a gawk that writes "S.S." after his name
with a flourish is in blissful ignorance of the fact that
instead of Secret Sorrow it may mean Sorry Sucker.

As I say, I held the Hudson River title undisputed for
eight years, and it's the hardest ground in the country to
cover properly. And with it all, I was—and am—a good
salesman. If you don't believe me, ask The Dillbecker
Company, Office Furniture, 543 Broadway.

The rice and old shoe thing never appealed to me. I
never even took the trouble to joke about it. My idea was
that marriage is a coeducational institution whose problems have no answer in the back of the book, whose lectures are given just when you want to sleep, and whose
course of painful instruction is finished only when the
minister stretches his hands over you palms downward,
and your friends and family throw on a few tears and nice
little bunches of flowers inscribed "Rest in peace."

For twelve long and happy years I harbored this amiable opinion of the tie that binds. I was a half-and-half
mixture of Benedick and Lothario, and I was never able

to decide which I admired the more. My convictions were impregnable. Women, I agreed, are the most delightful creatures in the world; I would rather be an S.S. than a Ph.D. any day. But no woman should ever tie me down to the "where have you been" thing; no woman should ever rope me in to teach me the hateful mysteries of a four-room flat; no woman should ever——

Then it hit me.

It happened in a little village not more than fifty miles north of Albany. I'd made a bum sale to the only furniture firm in town, and had gone out to Blank's house for dinner and to spend the evening. The first thing I saw when I entered the parlor was a little blue angel sitting at the piano.

"Who's that?" I asked my friend.

"My cousin," said she, "from Burlington."

We went into dinner almost immediately, and for the first time in my life I felt indifferent in the presence of food. The cousin sat across the table from me. I'm no describer, but I'll try to give you an idea of how she looked. She wore something blue with little bunches of lace at the wrists and neck. Her hands were so white they made her pink fingertips look almost red. Her eyes and lips seemed to belong to a sort of mutual benefit society. I never saw such perfect teamwork. They teased and trembled and tempted, and yet all the time they kept saying: "Never—absolutely never. We're having a lot of fun, but we will never——"

"You will!" I said aloud.

"You will what?" my friend asked coldly. She had been watching me. I was too busy to answer.

After dinner I walked out on the front porch alone. My eyes felt funny and I couldn't swallow. All over my chest it felt like someone was sticking needles in me and pulling them out again. I started down the steps, sat down on the top one, and began to review my past life. Then I jumped up and started to walk up and down the porch.

"Frank Keeler," said I, "you're sick. Your stomach's out of order. It's even possible that you're drunk. But don't you dare to tell me—" I clenched my teeth hard— "don't you *dare* tell me——"

Then I went back into the house and sat and listened to her eyes for three wonderful hours.

We were married in September—the 28th, to be exact. At that, I kept my word. She didn't tie me down or rope me in. It was all I could do to get her to hold on to the rope after I tied it around my own neck. Before she'd even look at me, I had to admit that without her my life would be devoted to the joyless gloom of unrelieved masculinity.

We took a thirty-day wedding trip to Florida, then came to New York and rented a Harlem flat—she calls it an apartment. By that time my firm was sending me daily hints to the effect that although marriages may last forever, honeymoons don't; and on the Monday following I left on a trip upstate. My wife's mother had come down a day or two before for a long visit, so it wasn't as though I was leaving her all alone among strangers.

In the short space of four months I had backed up, turned around and started off in the opposite direction. You've read how "in that one brief moment was condensed the experience of years, and from being a happy carefree girl she became suddenly a mature and resolute woman." Well, as a quick-change artist "she" didn't have anything on me. I had become the most faithful and devoted husband south of the North Pole.

In this, you understand, I was serious—darned serious. If I thought you'd know what I mean, I'd say I was an extremist. Of course I don't claim any originality; many a man has called the Venus de Milo ugly because she didn't look like his wife. But usually it's merely a disease. With me it amounted to a religion. And there wasn't any forcing about it, either; the thing actually seemed to agree with me. The worst of it was, I liked it.

As I say, soon after edging into a Harlem flat I left for upstate. The parting was tender and tearful. It was the first time I'd ever left for the front looking backward, and as I ran into an ash cart while turning to throw a final kiss up at the window where my wife sat, I felt for an instant that life had been robbed of one of its sweetest pleasures. But by the time I'd reached the 125th Street Station and bought a mileage book, I was thinking how dignified and noble it was to go out into the world and work for the support of a wife and the preservation of a home.

I shall never forget that trip up and down the river. I had never before realized the full extent of my success and popularity. If I told you all the incidents of that eventful month it would sound like the plot of a musical comedy or the autobiography of a jackass. At each stop it seemed as though everybody I didn't want to see was waiting for me at the station.

I'd got no farther than Peekskill when I discovered that no man should ever become a Secret Sorrow unless he intends to stick on the job. If you tell a woman she's all the world to you, she's usually willing enough to let you fall off the earth; but if you can get her to put her hand in yours just once, and then tell her how sad it makes you to feel that you can never love her, she'll never let go. If you say you love her, she yawns indifferently and asks what time it is; if you say you *can't* love her she looks at you dreamy and sad and makes you promise to stay over an extra day on your spring trip. Multiply that by 249 and you'll have some idea of what I was up against.

It wouldn't have mattered so much if I'd been willing to sit tight in the front parlor and explain things. But nothing like that for me. You'll get an inkling of my state of mind when I tell you that I cut out Harris & Puler at Troy because they've got a lady buyer who always expects a box of candy and a pleasant smile. Each morning I said over to myself a Lord Tennyson vow about faithfulness in word, thought and deed, and I was getting better every day. I figured that if I came through that first trip with a whole skin the rest would be plain sailing; and what with going down side streets and taking the first train out of towns and spending my Sundays in places where I'd never left my mark, I was exceeding my own fondest hopes.

Every night I wrote a long letter to my wife, full of lonesomeness. Hers were a little more cheerful. She and her mother were picking all the department stores to pieces and filling the flat with everything from pillows to pills; and at the end of my third week out she wrote me that her brother was in New York for a few days and had already invited them to two concerts and four plays. It was in the same letter that she told me about tying a pink ribbon on the sponge in my humidor. It didn't make me feel any better to know that she could be gay and happy while I was lonesome and homesick—to say nothing of the awful temptations I was dodging—but still I knew that was better than if she was there all alone. And of course I didn't complain any. Instead, I wrote her to be sure and have her brother stay till I got back, so I could show him a corner or two which he'd probably miss without a guide.

By this time I was going along pretty easy. The worst territory had all been covered, and I'd proved my mettle by steering straight between Scylla and Charybdis without blinking an eye. I had only a week more to go, and I began to breathe easy and natural, feeling that all danger was past. I even got so cheerful and gay that I wrote my wife I wouldn't arrive till Saturday, thinking to get in on Thursday and give her a little surprise.

Thursday morning I called on Marshall Bros. of Poughkeepsie—my last stop. I'd been selling them for ten years, and I knew that all I had to do was to run over the stock and fill in the empty places. So I went back to the office and got Billy and we had the job finished up in an hour. Then I went to the office again to get the order signed.

Just as I got ready to leave old man Marshall came in, looking worried. As he caught sight of me his face brightened up.

"Keeler," he said, "you're just the man I want. When do you leave?"

"Twelve fifteen for New York," said I, "and as fast as I can go."

"Couldn't be better," said he. "Come in here a minute."

Now I'm always willing and anxious to oblige a customer, of course. So when I followed him into his private office I walked eager and pleasant. Then he explained to me that his wife's niece was going down to New York to visit a cousin, and she was very innocent and timid and had never been there before, and would I act as escort?

I don't know exactly how to describe my sensations when he finished. What good had it done me to spend most of my time in dark alleys and bum hotels? What good had it done me to throw away the advantages and perquisities of twelve years' hard work and experience? What good had it done me to fill up with Henry Van Dyke and the Ladies' Home Companion? What good had it done me if at the very end I was to have a young, timid innocent niece set right down in the same seat with me for a two hour-trip down the Hudson?

All of which isn't as foolish as it sounds. I know my weakness. Like Lord Darlington, I can resist everything except temptation.

I felt that I had just one chance. There are nieces and nieces. As I packed my sample case I kept hoping that she would prove to be a second, or even a run of the mill.

She wasn't. She was the kind that comes in a case by itself, packed in cotton and invoiced separately. As I shook hands with her on the station platform I took a wild and despairing grip on my Lord Tennyson vow. Then I realized that I was gripping her hand even harder, and I dropped it and went over to the baggage room to read

over the last letter from my wife. I got back just in time
to help her on the train and shake hands with old man
Marshall.

We hadn't gone a mile before she asked me to lay her
coat up on the rack, and thanked me in that way that says:
"I'm so glad *you* were here to do that for me." Then I
reversed the seat in front, and she put one foot up on it—
the one next the window. It was only about half covered
by a low, small, dainty pump, and the ankle and its surroundings were composed entirely of curves. She turned
clear around in the seat and sat facing me. Her hair was
a kind of reddish brown—different from any I'd ever
seen—and it kept trying to crawl out from under her hat.
Her eyes, big and brown, had a tender, friendly look that
seemed willing to admit anything, and her mouth—

Then I went to the other end of the car for a drink of
water.

The incidents of that two-hour ride are still sort of hazy
in my memory. Of course for any ordinary man it would
have been simple and easy, but all the time I had a re-
membrance of my previous record, my promises to my
wife, and a perfume that blew over from the niece's hair
whirling around before me in a sort of Donnybrook Fair.
I was afraid even to be polite, and I guess she had begun
to think I was the original and only genuine clam. Then—
this was about at Tarrytown—after trying hard for thirty
minutes, I managed to say something about my wife.

"Are you *married?*" said she, like that.

I nodded. She looked at me interested for a minute, and
then said:

"Poor man!"

"I don't agree with your sentiment," said I with some
heat. "I'm the luckiest man in the world. The true state
of happiness is—"

"Freedom." She shook her head again and laughed.
"That's why I intend to hold on to it as long as I can."

Than I thanked God I'd told her I was married. If I

hadn't, I never would have been able to pass by such a challenge as that. Even as it was I felt an awful longing to make her take it back. No man who thinks anything of his sex or has any self-respect can allow a woman to go around talking about freedom, especially when she's pretty.

"I hate to be personal," she went on presently, "but can you see anything in this car, for instance, that is apt to make a girl long for a plain gold band and a six foot veil?"

I turned and looked straight at her, and found her laughing at me. "Miss Robinson," I said, "your uncle told me you were innocent and timid. If he could only—"

"I *am*," she interrupted. "I didn't say a word till I discovered you were harmless."

Good God! I—Frank Keeler—harmless! And it was true. That was the worst of it. It was true. I turned away from her with a bitter smile, and began to wonder if she had any idea of my pace under an empty saddle. Then I went to the smoking car and sat there talking to myself clear to Grand Central Station.

Her cousin lived up on Washington Heights, so it would have been quicker to get off at 125th Street, but I was too busy with my reflections to think about it. I managed to steer her through about four miles of scaffoldings and boardwalks, and I noticed it was just half-past two as we boarded a subway express for uptown. I counted on getting home by four.

By the time we got off at 168th Street I was pretty well calmed down. Although it made me unhappy to realize that I'd just been forced to swallow a gross insult to my long training and unquestioned ability, and that all the rest of my life I'd be helpless in the face of the strongest provocation, I could yet remember with pride the day when "Frank" was a household word in a hundred towns. And I felt a kind of pity come over me as I looked at the niece and reflected that she'd never know what she'd missed.

Consequently, I was feeling almost sad as we turned in a marble entrance on 168th Street, and told the elevator boy to take us to Robinson's apartment.

"They ain't in," said he, as if he was glad of it. "Gone out of town for a week."

They'd left four days before. He didn't know where they'd gone. The niece and I sat down in the hall to talk it over.

"Didn't they know you were coming?" I asked.

"No," she said. "I was going to surprise them."

I remembered that I had planned a surprise too, so I couldn't very well blame her. She said she didn't want to go back to Poughkeepsie unless she had to, but she didn't want to cause me any more bother. Of course I said she was anything but that. Then she said she had another cousin in New York, and she might go there.

"Just the thing!" I cried. "Where does she live?"

"Bath Beach," replied the niece calmly, just as though she was stating a pleasant fact instead of a horrible dream.

Well, there was only one thing to do. I didn't stop to explain what I was about to suffer for her sake, nor what she was up against herself. I thought she'd find out soon enough.

We took a subway express downtown again, got off at Brooklyn Bridge and with the help of three policeman and a cripple found an L train for Bath Beach. As we started out from the terminal I wondered if I would ever get back. Even a Harlem flat looks like a real home, sweet home to a man when he gets lost in the wilderness.

We'd been under way about twenty minutes when the niece turned to me looking puzzled.

"What place is this?" she asked. "It's so—funny. It seems that I've seen it in a dream."

"It must have been a nightmare," said I. "Don't talk so loud. This is Brooklyn."

For miles and miles, and it seemed hours and hours, we sat there in silence, waiting for the end. Finally the guard called out "Bath Beach!" and we jumped off onto a pile of ashes and tin cans. Then, after waiting a quarter of an hour for a trolley car that didn't come, we started off down the street.

I gave a sigh of relief as I went up the steps of a brown and green two-story house and rang the bell. Almost immediately the door opened, and the niece started forward, then fell back again as she caught sight of the old dried up woman that looked through at her.

"Is this Robinson's?" I asked.

"Naw," she said. The door slammed in my face.

I looked at the number over the door, then at the sign on the street corner, then at the niece. "This is 6123 Bath Avenue," I said sternly.

For answer she sat down on the porch step and began to cry. "I *thought* it was 6123," she said between sobs.

She got all right in a minute or two, and we started for the nearest drug store to look at a directory. Then she remembered that the Robinsons had moved down there only a few months ago, so the directory would be useless. She stopped and began to think.

"It might have been 6132," she said.

I left her at the drug store, and tried 6132, 6312, 6321, 6231 and 6213. Then I got desperate and went about three miles down to 3261. Just to save time and paper, figure out for yourself how many combinations there are in that damnable figure. I got back to the drug store about six o'clock.

"Nothing doing," I said, as friendly as I could. "There's no Robinsons in Bath Beach. There's only one thing to do. Come home with me. My wife'll be glad to have you."

The niece got ready to cry again. "But I can't," she said. "She doesn't know me."

"I can introduce you, can't I?" I demanded. "Unless you want to stay at a hotel." But I could see she wouldn't do that.

She was silent for a minute; then, "I'm going back to Poughkeepsie," she said. "When can I get a train?"

I could see she meant it, and besides, I realized it was the best thing to do. So I didn't waste any time in argument.

On the trip back my spirits jumped a notch every time the wheels went round. It was a combination of relief and expectation that I can't exactly define. I suppose I should have had a premonition, but I know I didn't.

At Grand Central we found out that the next train to Poughkeepsie was at 8:20. I looked at the niece. She was leaning against the window rail and seemed kind of limp.

"That's an hour," she said, glancing at the clock.

"Yes," said I. "What's the matter? Don't you feel well?" She was gazing across the room in a kind of trance. Looking in the same direction I saw a big double door, and over the top the word "Restaurant."

Of course I should have thought of it sooner, but I'd been so darned busy looking for Robinsons I hadn't had time for anything else.

"Good Lord!" I exclaimed. "We haven't had anything to eat since morning!"

"Yesterday," she said. "I never eat breakfast."

Instinctively we started together for the big double doors. About halfway across I suddenly stopped. "Listen," I said. "We have a full hour. Why not go to a *good* place? It's close."

"Anywhere," said the niece. "But I don't want to miss the train."

Why I chose Rector's I don't know. But I did. It was pretty well crowded but we found a table over on the Broadway side, and I ordered everything I could recognize.

The companionship of the knife and fork has always appealed to me. I suppose that's what made me feel so friendly; but there were other considerations. When two people go to Brooklyn together they are forever bound by a sort of mutual sympathy. Also, I felt grateful to her for going back to Poughkeepsie instead of coming home with me. So by the time we'd finished with the roast we were almost chummy. It had even got to the place where I was trying to show her the advantages of being married. When I got through she stretched a hand across the table to me.

"Mr. Keeler," she said, "I believe you. I really don't know anything about it, but I'll take your word for it. And after all your kindness to me, I'd like to congratulate the girl that was lucky enough to get you. I'd like to meet your wife."

Suddenly she stopped and looked up. So did I. Two women and a man had stopped on their way out and were looking down at us. It was my wife, her mother and her brother.

If you expected to hear a good story, of course you're disappointed. There isn't even any use explaining to you that I've spent five months trying to explain it to my wife, and she won't listen.

I've been a Secret Sorrow, I've been a Faithful Husband, and I've been a Fool. As I hinted before, if you want to make me believe that Carrie Nation smashed a joint, you've got to show me the hole in the window.

I'm going to give my wife just one more chance. I'm going to write it all out, have it typewritten, and maybe have it printed in a magazine. Then if she don't believe it—well, the niece is still at Poughkeepsie, and as I said before, no man who has any self-respect can allow a pretty woman to go around talking about freedom.

ANNUNCIO'S VIOLIN

A nnuncio lay peacefully sleeping in the shade of a scrub mesquite. Now and again a curious, errant mud dauber, adventure-bent, explored the mazes of his wavy, ebony hair, or viewed from the vantage point of nose or chin the offerings of the surrounding country. Anon, a giant, home-returning ant, holding aloft a world of stolen grain for winter use, crawled across the bare, hemp-sandaled feet. But Annuncio still dreamed on. In easy reach of his brown-fingered hand, which yet retained half-lovingly the aged bow lay, dusty on the earth, an old violin, whose gracious curves and simple elegance of form revealed the master workman's craft. Annuncio's grandsire himself knew little of its history or of how the instrument had come to them, save only that his own father had played him to sleep in childhood with the self-same bow. And now Annuncio played and dreamed, and waked to play again upon its ancient strings the lullabies and love songs of his people.

Within the low, thatch-roofed adobe house nearby, Eulalia began at last the preparation of their evening meal, humming low to herself as she ground the maize in the stone bowl and formed the cakes for baking. Eulalia was not as happy with her ardent wooing lover as she had thought to be. No poet she. To her, life meant more than dreaming through the sunny day and playing half-forgotten love songs to the tropic stars at night. Hers was the daily task of managing the little household cares, buying their scant supplies, and bargaining for all their simple, homely wrought apparel. And so it was that the wife had come to be the real ruler of the home, whom Annuncio indulged in every whim if only he might be allowed to dream and play. But poor Eulalia was not content with all this homage. She loved the bright mantillas of her richer sisters in the town, and gazed with longing that was not wholly free from envy at the *coche* and four white, prancing horses of Las Esperanzes' mayor whenever that dignitary passed by on a visit to some neighboring ranch.

The first cool evening breeze came wandering down from the mountain and wakened Annuncio. Sitting up, he raised the violin for an ante-supper melody. And while he played, slowly, unnoticed along the road approached a man, at once a *gringo* and a *vaga-bundo*. Attracted as much, perhaps, by the sweetness of the melody he heard as by the savory odor of *tortillas* coming from the house, the stranger left the highway and drew near the spot where Annuncio was sitting. With a single glance he appraised the ordinary surroundings of the peon's home, but when his eyes, furtive and shifting, rested on the native's violin, a new interest dawned in them.

The tune ended, Annuncio rose, aware for the first time of the stranger's presence. The latter showed a small coin and asked for supper and a place to sleep. Annuncio, eyeing with distrust the American's ragged clothes and unkempt exterior, began to refuse his hospitality, when Eulalia, coming out to fetch her man, caught sight of the *real* and bade the *gringo* enter.

The tortillas and frijoles eaten, Annuncio again took up his violin to play away the evening. The *gringo* listened for a space and then, turning to Annuncio, told him to bring the instrument close to the candle. Taking it from the reluctant hand of its owner, the *gringo* scrutinized the scratched and grimy case with half-concealed satisfaction. This done, he played, or rather wrenched from the unaccustomed strings, a few measures of Strauss' waltz, and handing back to miserable Annuncio his ravaged pet, he said: "My friends, I am a lonely man. On my travels often I need the music to urge my tired feet. This little violin could help me much. I wish you to sell me it for company."

Annuncio at once and firmly demurred. Eulalia, the discontented, desired to know what the Señor would give. The Señor had but five *pesos dos reales* by him in silver, but this would scarce suffice to pay them for so great a boon, the life-long friendship of the violin, and so, the Señor would—ah, what cared he for gold, he wished for companionship—they had each other, but he went all alone—would give them for their charity to him, a lonely wayfarer, a lottery ticket sure to win the grand prize of 10,000 *pesos*, sold him by a friendly officer of the lottery Nacional whom he had saved from drowning but last month. This would he give to them, his friends.

Annuncio thought of all the starry nights to come without the solace of a single melody, and sadly shook his head; Eulalia thought of all the glories of a *coche* and four white, prancing steeds, of soft laces, silver combs, and silken shawls, a house in town, servants—and smiling, nodded her assent.

"And we will buy you many new violeens, all cherry red and shining," whispered she to hesitating 'Nuncio, and so the bargain ended.

The tenth of August came and early in the morning Eulalia rose to furbish up the threadbare jacket and breeches of 'Nuncio. Today began the new life, for was not the grand prize already theirs, waiting now in Esperanzes for the presentation of the winning ticket. Of a certainty. And so 'Nuncio was to trudge the ten hot, dusty miles on foot, but to return—ah, that triumphant march, had not Eulalia dreamed it over a dozen times? To return proudly borne back the weary way in a *coche* drawn by four white, prancing horses, even as the worthy *corregidor* of the town. The fertile brain of Eulalia had planned it all. They would destroy all vestige of their former poverty in one grand offering to the kindly gods of chance. Together they piled all their meager household goods—the shaky table, the rude chairs, and all the rest—into a little hillock beneath the center of the thatched roof. Their little store of maize and coffee, too, were placed thereon, and flung atop the heap lay whatever clothes they had other than those they wore. No single thing of all their former state would they retain. A little brush-wood fire smouldered without the door, and from this Eulalia, at first glimpse of returning *coche* and four, would take a brand and kindle that within. So they had planned and so it was to be.

Two o'clock saw 'Nuncio, dusty and worn, enter the main street of Esperanzes, the *Calle Alvarez*. Easily he found the office of the Nacional and entered, smiling round the crowd of loiterers standing by the door. In one minute the prize would be his, and he the richest man in many kilometers around. He stepped to the desk and presented the worn, tattered ticket.

"My ten thousand *pesos, si gusta*."

The clerk smiled affably.

"The ticket is two years old, *pobrecito*," he said, "and wasn't worth a *centava* even then."

"But the Señor said"—began 'Nuncio pleadingly.

The clerk only nodded pleasantly toward the door and commenced to talk to the little stenographer.

Annuncio stumbled to the sidewalk and started slowly away. He thought dazedly of his long journey home on foot and of the sad news he must tell his wife. Someone gave him a *peseta* and bade him get a drink. He went to a nearby store and purchased a bottle of mezcal, stupidly wondering if the Señor would ever bring back his precious violin, now that the lottery ticket was no good. Surely so kind a man as the Señor would not keep a poor man's property if he knew.

Thus sorrowfully musing, Annuncio wandered to the edge of town and took up the long way back to Eulalia. But now the road seemed strangely long to his tired feet. He began to resort to frequent drinks from the bottle. After a time he sat down to rest by the roadside. Some vehicle was coming from the city. Maybe they were coming after him to say that there had been some mistake. Or perhaps it was the mail *coche* to San Luis. Then he recognized the mayor's equipage. Ah yes, 'Nuncio remembered this was the evening of the grand *baile* at Madero's, and doubtless the Señor Corregidor was overtaking him on his way thither. And would the Señor be so kind as to give him a lift, being very tired with the long walk? Of a certainty the Señor would. 'Nuncio might get up on the seat with the driver.

Thankfully he did so, and the *coche* proceeded toward the Madero ranch, the hacienda next beyond his own humble adobe. Little by little 'Nuncio's body relaxed, lulled by the easy rolling *coche*, and soon he forgot the troubles of the day, lost in a half-dream of near-forgotten melodies.

But suddenly, in front of them, through the gathering dusk of the autumn evening, a glorious, scarlet burst of flame leaped quivering into the air. Annuncio started up.

"Jesus Maria," he said, dully, "our little plan!"

THE INFERNAL FEMININE

Young Stafford devoted a full hour to the note, and even then was unable to satisfy himself. It was the ninth draft that he finally decided to send, and he folded it and sealed the envelope with the air of a philosopher who realizes how far short of the perfect are our most earnest endeavors. The note read as follows:

Dear Miss Blair:

I have been in New York two months; just long enough to form a decision that it is for the most part an exceedingly over-praised institution. Then, last night, a friend took me to see "Winning Winona," and the moment you appeared on the stage that decision was reversed.

I shall not apologize for the informality of this; if you are inclined to be offended it would be useless. I shall only say that I wish very much to have the pleasure of meeting you, and that, having studied you for two hours, I know you will at least be kind enough to accept my best and most tender regards and wishes.

> Yours sincerely,
> Arnold Stafford.

Now, despite this evidence to the contrary submitted in black and white, Arnold Stafford was a sensible youth. There comes a time in the life of every man when he feels an overwhelming impulse to send a note to a musical comedy soubrette; and it is no credit to him if he is too cowardly or too cautious to yield to it. And when the soubrette happens to be Betty Blair—well, have you ever seen her?

As for the merit of the note itself, it must be admitted that it was a rather curious performance. It had a curtness and brevity that was almost legal—which perhaps was an effect intended deliberately. Anyway, it must be remembered that Stafford was wholly without experience in the matter.

The important thing is, it produced results. It was the third morning after sending his note that Stafford found in his mail a gray, severe envelope. Tearing it open, he read as follows:

> Dear Mr. Stafford—You may meet me—if you will—at the stage door after the performance on Friday evening.
>
> > Sincerely,
> > Betty Blair.

If Stafford had been a member of that gilded brotherhood which impedes the traffic of Broadway without any apparent purpose other than to prove that an animal with two legs is not necessarily a man, this seeming compliance on the part of Miss Blair would have filled him with suspicion. But as he was merely a promising young lawyer, with more or less of an excuse for existence, he was only pleased and a little surprised. As he attempted to convey to his tailor some idea of the importance of the occasion for which certain repairs were necessary, he realized that he was getting considerably more than he had dared to expect.

On Tuesday evening he went again to see "Winning Winona," also, on Wednesday and Thursday. He was forced to miss the Wednesday matinée only by a business engagement, which it was impossible to postpone, and yet the dawning of Friday saw, if anything, an increase of his impatience and eagerness. That is what raised Stafford's whim to the dignity of passion. An infatuation that can withstand four performances of a popular Broadway show is not a thing to be regarded lightly, as an invitation to supper or a wedding engagement. It approaches the divine.

As is entirely proper in such cases, Stafford harbored no serious intentions. He was not entirely unsophisticated, and he knew very well that one goes to supper with an actress just as he goes to dinner with an appetite, or to church with a Bible. It is true that he was finding it difficult to reconcile this approved viewpoint with his own tumultuous feelings and eager expectation, but he accounted for the difference on the charge of novelty, and gave his undivided attention to the arrangement of his toilet and the choice of a restaurant.

Friday's performance of Broadway's newest hit, though in reality sadly similar to all the others, seemed to Stafford to be invested with a particular charm and freshness. That was due to the fact that he took no notice of it whatever; his mind was entirely occupied with wild admiration of Betty Blair when she was on the stage, and restless impatience when she wasn't. He felt a sort of pity mingled with superiority, for the rest of the audience, who had to be content with their seats in the fifth row—or the fifteenth, which was worse—and share the glances of the divine Betty with anyone who had two dollars and a distaste for music. Then, reflecting that such a sentiment hardly suited a blasé man of the world—which role he had definitely decided to assume—he spent the entire third act in the lobby, smoking cigarettes and looking as tired as possible.

He carefully avoided all appearance of haste. As the audience emerged from the theater he leaned against a nearby pillar and surveyed them, individually and collectively, with a cold and cheerless eye. Then he sauntered leisurely around to the stage door—and noted with alarm that members of the company were already leaving. He approached the guardian of the door and addressed him in a voice of anxiety.

"Has Miss Blair come out yet?"

The man in uniform eyed him a moment impassively, then his face brightened up. "Miss Blair? What is your name, please."

Stafford handed him a card, and he disappeared in the narrow hall. A minute passed—two—then out into the white blaze of the arc over the entrance came Miss Betty Blair, with a dainty step and an entrancing swish. As Stafford advanced to meet her, hat in hand, she looked up inquiringly, smiled sweetly and said, in a silvery April-shower voice:

"Mr. Stafford? I'm *so* pleased to meet you."

Those persons who are inclined to regard Stafford unfavorably, from whatever viewpoint, would do well to remember that the lure of the actress has been felt by more than one man worthy of the name, from Louis the Fourteenth down—or up—to Richard Le Gallienne. Her only business is to be charming, her only care is to entertain, her only desire is to please; for the public, of course. And thrice happy is the man who is able, even for one brief hour, to monopolize those melting glances, those musical tones and those pretty gestures! Studied or ingenuous, it matters not; they are there, and they are irresistible. Besides, do we not hear the man at the next table tell his companion that "that is Betty Blair?"

Such was the delightful tenor of Stafford's reflections as he led the way to a table in the tastefully subdued supper room at the Vanderbilt. It was, as he had hoped it would be, crowded. The soft carpets caressed his feet; a Viennese waltz sounded in his ears; the second glances at Betty Blair filled his heart with pride and his chest with wind. He motioned the waiter aside and himself adjusted her chair and arranged her cape. Then, after giving their order, he sat and regarded her expectantly, still scenting vaguely the delicious perfume that had arisen from her crown of golden brown hair.

"I'm not going to ask *why* you're so kind to me," he said. Betty Blair sat silent, pulling off her gloves.

"What do reasons amount to at a time like this?" continued Stafford. "It's enough to know that we are here. Outside is the world, with its sorrows and its pain, its cold logic and its stubborn facts. No one knows better than I how full it is of shams and lies and hypocrisy. It is only when his heart speaks that a man tells the truth."

"And you?"

"Mine is speaking now. It has been—ever since I first saw you. If I could only tell you all that I have felt—all that these few days have meant to me! I have thought of nothing else, I have cared for nothing else, but this." His tone was full of earnestness, his eyes looked into hers with a sincere and real appeal.

"But you don't expect me to believe you?"

"Try me," Stafford leaned forward and spoke eagerly. "I know what you would say: that I do not know you. Ah! Do I not? Who could look into your eyes without seeing the kindness of your heart? Nothing could make me happier than that you should ask me for proof. Anything—I would do anything."

A smile, charming and earnest, appeared on the face of

Betty Blair. She stretched a hand across the table toward
Stafford. Her eyes looked into his with confidence and
satisfaction.

"I believe you," she said, "because I want to. But I'm
going to demand your proof."

"I would do anything, go anywhere for you," repeated
Stafford, as gravely as his intoxication would permit. "A
demand from you is a favor. Try me."

Betty Blair opened a large silk bag which she had carried on her arm, and from it took a long slip of paper, a
leather bound tablet and a fountain pen. She turned a cool,
calculating eye on Stafford, unsheathed the fountain pen,
and cleared her throat in a businesslike manner.

"Your address is 25 Broad Street?"

Stafford, guessing wildly as to the meaning of these
deliberate preparations, nodded.

Betty Blair turned to a page in the leather bound book
and wrote on it. Then:

"You are a Republican, I believe?"

"Unless you're a Democrat."

"Mr. Stafford, this is no joke. You *are* a Republican?"

"I am," seriously. "Is it a crime?"

For reply Betty Blair pushed the slip of paper across
the table and handed him the fountain pen. "Sign on the
twenty-fourth line, please," she said.

As Stafford caught up the paper and read the printed
paragraph at the top his jaw became firmly set and his
hand trembled. Then he looked across at Betty Blair with
a cold and cheerless eye.

"Miss Blair," he said, "I congratulate you. But you've
missed your mark. I refuse to keep a promise obtained by
fraud and misrepresentation."

"Mr. Stafford!"

"O piffle!" said the exasperated Stafford inelegantly.
"You've deceived me. You've destroyed my illusions. But
you're up against the wrong man. Take it from me, the
best thing you can do is to put a marble bust of Sappho

on your mantelpiece, read carefully the life of Peg Woffington and hang Susan B. Anthony on a sour apple tree. If you've finished supper I'm ready to go."

"Mr. Stafford," Betty Blair's voice was cold and stern, "this is no time for personalities. Can you deny that 'Votes for Women' is the universal password in the intellectual world of today? I'm not surprised that you wouldn't sign that pledge, even after you'd promised. It's just like a man. But I warn you—" she choked with indignation— "I warn you——"

"You have already," Stafford rose and laid a bill on his plate. Then, as he turned to go, "Never again for me," he said bitterly. "An hour ago I was thanking God I'd found you. Now I'm thankful I found you out—before it was too late. Oh, I know what a real woman is—or ought to be. I read about one once in a novel. I had no idea they'd gone so far as to demoralize the stage."

That was all. An hour later Stafford was uneventfully and comfortably lying lonesome but safe in his bachelor bed. The only really important thing about the story is its application. As Stafford himself expressed it a day or two later, it's a waste of time to search for live specimens of an extinct species.

A PROFESSIONAL RECALL

They met at Quinby's unexpectedly, for the first time in three months, and after the handshake proceeded to their old table in the corner.

"Well, how goes it?" asked Bendy.

"Bendy," said Dudd Bronson, ignoring the question, "I am the greatest man in the world. I myself am for ham and cabbage, since it tickles my feelings, but if you want anything from peacocks' hearts to marmalade, it's on me."

Bendy stared at the roll of bills Dudd brought out of his trousers' pocket. "Dudd," he said, his voice trembling, "I respect you. Please put it in your breast pocket so I can see the bulge. What was the occurrence?"

"I hate to tell it," declared Dudd. "Bendy, I am a modest man. When you admire me most, remember I said that.

"The pity of it is that there was no one to watch me. I done it in solitude.

"One day, about two weeks ago, I walks into the sanctum of David Jetmore. Jetmore is the best lawyer in Horton, over in Jersey. He's one of them fat, bulgy men that looks right through you with a circumambious gaze.

" 'Mr. Jetmore,' says I, 'my name is Abe Delman. I been running a store over in Pauline with my brother Leo. We had a fight over a personal matter which ain't to the purpose, and when Leo began lookin' for me in an unpeaceful manner I came away for my health. Now I want to get my half of the store which I am broke till I get it, and you should write to Leo's lawyer, who is Mr. Devlin of Ironton, about a settlement.'

" 'Have you something for a retainer?' asks Jetmore.

" 'No,' says I, 'I'm livin' at a hotel.'

" 'I'm a busy man,' says Jetmore, 'and how do I know I'll get any money?'

" 'Mr. Jetmore,' says I, 'that store's worth three thousand dollars if it's worth a cent. And if my half ain't enough, maybe you can get Leo to give you some of his.'

"Finally, after I explained promiscuously why I had to keep at an unsafe distance from brother Leo, and other delicate points, Jetmore says he'll take the job. When he says Devlin, Leo's lawyer in Ironton, is a personal friend of his, I told him that made it all the better, but I had a mental reserve about the *espree dee corpse*.

"That same afternoon about four hours later I walks into Devlin's office in Ironton.

" 'Mr. Devlin,' says I, 'my name is Leo Delman. I been running it a store over in Pauline with my brother Abe. We had a fight over a personal matter which ain't to the purpose, and Abe left for parts unknown without my blessing. Two days ago comes a letter from Abe's lawyer, Mr. Jetmore of Horton, about Abe's share in the store, which he didn't wait to take with him, and I told him to write to you, because you should make it a settlement for me.'

"Bendy, these lawyers is all the same. All they think about is what's in it for them. They're parasites, Bendy. They're a menace to society.

" 'Have you something for a retainer?' asks Devlin.

" 'Mr. Devlin,' says I, 'I have not.'

" 'Then,' says he, 'how do you expect to settle with brother Abe?'

"Bendy, I know you won't repeat this to any of our friends, or I wouldn't tell it. It fills me with shame, Bendy, when I remember that fifty I handed to Devlin. These lawyers is the worst kind of grafters.

"I told Devlin I didn't want any Pauline natives to know about mine and Abe's intimate pertinacities, and I waits in Ironton for a settlement. As soon as he got my fifty he wrote off a long letter to Jetmore which he let me read to correct the sentiments.

"It would a' been cheaper for me to buy that railroad between Ironton and Horton. For eleven days I kept up a to and fro movement worse than a Mount Vernon commuter. It got so the trains wouldn't start till they saw me comin'. In one day I was Abe three times and Leo twice.

"Jetmore and Devlin kept burnin' up the mails with lies and criminalities, me a readin' everything so as to preserve my interests. I was yellin' for more on one end and less on the other till the fruit got all ripe and just ready for pickin'. Bendy, it was shameful easy, I used to fall asleep in Devlin's office from sheer *angwee*.

"It was last Thursday when I got to Devlin's sanctum just in time to see him puttin' on his coat to go to lunch with the stenographer.

" 'Hello, Delman,' says he, 'I'll see you in about half an hour. Here's a letter from Jetmore. Make yourself at home till I get back.'

"When he'd gone I read the letter over just to make sure there wasn't no changes since I saw it the night before in Jetmore's office. It said that Abe had decided to accept Leo's offer of twelve hundred dollars cash, provided it was paid within three days.

"I goes to the stenographer's desk, picks out a nice printed letterhead, and writes on it as follows:

March 21, 1912

Mr. David Jetmore,
Horton, N. J.
Dear Sir,

As per advice contained in your favor of the 20th inst., I am enclosing herewith check for twelve hundred dollars in full payment of the claim of Abe Delman against Leo Delman.

I shall be pleased to have you acknowledge receipt of same.

Yours very truly,

"I had already practiced Devlin's hand till I was sick of it, and I signed that letter so that Devlin himself couldn't a' told the difference. Then I pulls out a blank check, makes it to the order of Devlin for twelve hundred dollars and signs it 'Leo Delman' and endorses Devlin's name on the back.

"Of course, I could have done some of this work in my own boodwar, but I wanted to use Devlin's typewriter, and besides, I had a feeling it would be more gentlemanlike to do everything right there in the office. It somehow seemed natural and right to sign a man's name on his own desk with his own pen and ink.

"When Devlin come back I had the letter all ready to mail stowed away in my pocket.

" 'Have you got that twelve hundred?' says he.

" 'No,' says I, 'but I'll get it in three days or bust.'

" 'You'd better,' says he, 'for when Jetmore says three days he don't mean four.'

"I mailed the letter and check in Ironton that afternoon, and next day—that was Friday—I goes over to Horton on the very first train, and pedestrinates into Jetmore's office on the stroke of ten.

"Jetmore met me cordial like a mule that's just found something to kick. He'd smelled my money.

" 'Did you get it?' says I.

"He pulled out the check I'd mailed in Ironton the day before. I looked at it over his shoulder, him holdin' on with both hands.

" 'I guess about fifty of that belongs to you,' says I.

" 'Fifty!' says he. 'Fifty!'

" 'No,' says I, 'I only said it once.'

"That's what comes of gettin' into the clutches of one of them grafters, Bendy. They'll do you every time. But I let it go at a hundred to preserve my own interests. I couldn't afford no argument.

" 'Well,' says I, 'give me the check.'

" 'Give me my hundred,' says he.

" 'I ain't got it,' says I.

" 'Then we'll cash the check,' says he, and puts on his coat and hat.

"Bendy, ain't that pitiful? Ain't it pitiful? It was comin' so easy I yawned right in his face. Says he, 'then we'll cash the check.' Oh, the big fat boob!

"We goes down to the bank, and Jetmore steps up to the window.

" 'Good morning, Mr. Jetmore,' says the teller, obsequies-like.

"Jetmore takes a pen, endorses the check, and passes it through the window.

" 'Give it to us in hundreds,' says he.

" 'Not for me,' says I, steppin' up. 'Make it twenties.' You know, Bendy, centuries is all right, but they ain't enough of 'em. They're too scarce to be safe.

"The teller counts out ten twenties, slaps 'em on top of a pile with a bandage on 'em, and shoves 'em through the window to Jetmore. He counts off five and I sticks the rest in my pocket.

" 'Better count 'em,' says Jetmore.

" 'I'll take a chance,' says I. "The young man looks honest.' The truth is, I was beginning to get the shivers. They always come on me when I feel the stuff.

"Me and Jetmore turned to go. Just as we reached the door I felt that pile of twenties jump right out of my pocket and slap me in the face. Standin' there lookin' at us was Devlin.

" 'Hello, Jetmore,' says he. 'Good morning, Mr. Delman.'

"Bendy, stand up. No man can sit unrespectful while I relate the sequence. It fills my eyes with tears to think of it. I've been a modest man, but this is too much for me. I must tell the truth.

"I was in a hole, all right, but I still had hold of the rope. I knew that Devlin thinks I'm Leo and Jetmore thinks I'm Abe, and as long as they didn't get a chance to chin on it I was safe.

" 'Mr. Devlin,' says I, 'I'm glad to see you. There's a little matter I want to ask you about.'

"Jetmore started to spout before Devlin could answer and I interspersed.

" 'It's an important matter,' says I, 'and I won't keep you long.'

"Devlin stood lookin' at us like he didn't understand. Of course, Jetmore knew I knew Devlin, because I'd told him he was mine and Leo's lawyer before the fight.

"Jetmore pulls out his watch and starts to go.

" 'I've got an appointment,' says he. 'I'll see you later. Drop around to the office about one.' Then he turns to me. 'Come in and say good-by,' says he, and off he goes.

"It took me about two minutes to explain to Devlin that I'd come up to Horton to try to get Jetmore to chop off a hundred on the settlement. Devlin laughed.

" 'Jetmore don't do no choppin',' says he.

" 'Right you are,' says I. 'He won't even give me no extra time.'

" 'What was it you wanted to ask me?' says he.

" 'Mr. Devlin,' says I, 'I'm a poor man. Whether I get that twelve hundred I don't know. But I got some friends in Pittsburgh what's got it, and if you'll let me have that fifty back for railroad fare I'll make it a hundred when I settle up.'

"Devlin blinked hard, and I thought he'd jumped it. But bein' a grafter, that hundred looked too good to lose. He pulls out a big black wallet, counts out five tens, and hands 'em to me careful-like.

" 'Delman,' says he, 'I know you're an honest man. I can tell it by your eyes. I feel sure you'll get the money.'

" 'Mr. Devlin,' says I, holdin' his hand in one hand and the fifty in the other, 'I *will* get the money.' And I leaves him standin' there in the bank, watchin' me through the window.

"Did you go to Pittsburgh?" asked Bendy.

"Bendy," said Dudd, "don't be factious in the presence of genius. You offend me."

"Forgive me," said Bendy, humbly. "Let me see the fifty, Dudd. I just want to touch it."

PAMFRET AND PEACE

*Pamfret was happy. To be back in the world again, to
feel once more that old sense of incompleteness—
what could be more delightful? He laughed aloud as he
recollected how Satan had warned him that the earth
might not prove so attractive after all.

For Pamfret was no ordinary mortal. In 1910 he had
died, and as he had done some things and left undone
some others, he had been sent with slight ceremony to the
land of darkness. Of his existence there we have no
knowledge, save that he found it somewhat darker and a
great deal more interesting than he had imagined. Nor do
we know the exact nature of the service he rendered the
Prince; but it was an important one, and Satan rewarded
him with ten years more of life. Pamfret was wildly grateful, and almost incurred the Prince's displeasure by his
eagerness to return to the world above. Once there he
forgot everything but the joy of mortality.

He was considerably surprised when he found that the

world had gotten as far as 1970. Sixty years! Everything, of course, was changed. But he felt that just to be alive was enough. It was really very silly of Satan to give him that vial, he thought—as if there were any chance of his wishing to return before the ten years ended.

It was noon of his first day. As he walked along Fifth Avenue and noted the many changes and additions, the absence of old landmarks and the encroachments of commercialism, he experienced little of that feeling of unreality he had expected. After all, it was only natural that there should be changes. The world does not stand still. At Forty-second Street he stopped at the library, and felt a strange pleasure in renewing old acquaintances on its shelves. Two blocks farther on he was delighted to find that Sherry's had remained faithful to its old corner, and congratulated himself that he had not yet lunched.

He passed through the outer hall into the dining room on the left, intending to find a table near the orchestra, but found that the place formerly set aside for the musicians had been rearranged and furnished for diners. When he had found a seat and summoned a waiter, "Is there no orchestra?" he asked.

The waiter looked surprised. "Certainly not."

"Why certainly?"

"But it would cause disagreement. Some people like music and some do not. But Monsieur is jesting?"

Pamfret could see no joke. But at least they still had a menu. "Bring me some clams."

"Yes, sir."

"And some cold turkey with jelly."

"Yes, sir."

"And—have you any alligator pears?"

"No, sir."

"Well, then Salad Macedoine, and a pot of coffee."

"Yes, sir," and the waiter hurried away.

"That waiter has no imagination," thought Pamfret. "He had not a single suggestion to offer." And he leaned back in his chair the better to watch the crowd.

There was a curious air of calm about the room. Everyone was talking, but no one seemed at all interested in what anyone said. There was no animation, nothing of piquancy in either face or gesture. "What stupid people!" said Pamfret to himself.

Seated at the next table were a man and a girl. "I don't care to go," the girl was saying. "I adore opera but I hate plays."

"I have heard that this is a very good play, and I shall go," said the man.

"Very well, then I shall return home. Goodby," and she rose to go.

"Oh, are you finished?" asked the man. "All right. Goodby."

Pamfret was astonished. "The girl is pretty and the man is a fool," he declared; but the arrival of his waiter with a plate of clams put a stop to his soliloquy.

Three o'clock found Pamfret seated in the grandstand at the Polo Grounds. It was a day of glorious sunshine, and promised still more glorious sport. The old rivalry between New York and Chicago had been heightened by time, and the Cubs were even now battling with the Giants for first place. Pamfret felt a joyous excitement. He turned to his nearest neighbor. "The Giants are really the stronger team, aren't they?" he queried.

"That is a matter of opinion," replied his neighbor.

"Are you from Chicago?"

"No."

Pamfret subsided.

At three-thirty the game was called. "Now there'll be something doing," thought Pamfret.

The first inning passed quickly. The play was snappy,

but there were no runs made, and there was no applause. In the second inning Chicago's batters were soon disposed of. The first man up for New York drew a base on balls, and then—the next batter hit a triple to left, scoring the runner. The crowd was silent. Pamfret clapped his hands furiously.

An usher approached and handed Pamfret a printed card. Pamfret turned it over and read as follows:

INTERNATIONAL PEACE CONGRESS.

COMMITTEE ON ATHLETICS.

Rule 19. It shall be unlawful for a spectator at any athletic game to show preference to any contestant by any manner of applause or derision.

Pamfret was so bewildered that he forgot to watch the game. So that was the cause of this curious silence. He wondered what was the penalty, and decided, inasmuch as he was not disturbed further, that a warning was considered sufficient for a first offense.

Then he heard the crack of the bat against the ball, and looked just in time to see the little leather sphere bound against the left field fence and roll back onto the field. The runner tore wildly around the bases, while the crowd uttered not a sound. On past second he dashed, and rounded third just as the ball was being returned by the fielder. He flew down the home stretch with the speed of an arrow, and reached the plate the merest fraction of a second before the ball landed in the catcher's mitt.

"Out!" called the umpire.

"Robber!" shrieked Pamfret. "Thief! Robber!"

The crowd gazed at Pamfret in dismay. Again the usher approached and handed him a card. Pamfret, partially realizing what he had done, took it in a rather shamefaced manner, and read:

INTERNATIONAL PEACE CONGRESS.

COMMITTEE ON ATHLETICS.

Rule 26. It shall be unlawful for a spectator at any athletic game to show either approval or disapproval of any decision of the umpire or referee. Penalty: ejection from the grounds.

A silver gong sounded somewhere under the grandstand. Pamfret looked up. The entire mass of spectators was standing, each with bowed head and arm raised, pointing with outstretched finger to the outer gates. On the field each player had stopped still in his position and turned to point. Pamfret was confused; he wanted to laugh; but the air of solemnity about the whole proceeding forbade it. There could be no doubt about the meaning of this universal gesture, and he descended from the grandstand and started across the field toward the gates. As he arrived there, he turned and looked back. Thirty thousand fingers were pointing at him in a sort of contemptuous scorn. As he passed through the gates he heard the silver gong ring out as before.

"What the devil," he thought, as he boarded a downtown car, "is the world coming to? Or rather, what *has* the world come to? I don't believe I'm going to have such a good time after all"; and he sighed for the day when a close decision meant tears and threats unsurpassed even in Hell.

He began to long for someone to talk to—loneliness assailed him. A baby in the arms of a woman opposite him began to cry, and on a signal from the conductor the woman arose and left the car at the next corner. The man seated next to him—an awkward-looking man with a beard—was engaged in conversation with his neighbor on the other side. "The English," he was saying, "are a wonderful people."

"The Americans," replied the other, "are a very wonderful people."

"The English," said the bearded man, "are great artists."

"The Americans are a race of geniuses."

"The British Empire is indissoluble."

"America is the Land of Freedom."

"England is the greatest country in the world."

"Rule 142," said the American, calmly. "No comparisons allowed in an argument."

"I beg your pardon," said the Englishman.

But Pamfret was already on his feet. He had always hated the English. "Argument!" he shouted. "Argument! Do you call that an argument? Tell him he lies!"

"Rules 207, 216, and 349," said the Englishman and American in unison. "No contradictions, no personalities, and no loud talking."

The conductor touched Pamfret on the arm and signalled him to leave the car. Pamfret's first impulse was to throw him through a window; this continual restraint was becoming irksome. But he thought better of it, and besides, they had reached Sixty-sixth Street. He alighted at the next corner, and started south on Central Park West.

At Sixty-fifth Street was a restaurant, and he stopped for dinner. The room was crowded; but finally Pamfret found a table over against the wall, sat down and called a waiter, who seemed a little worried as he caught sight of him.

"Table d'hote?" asked Pamfret.

"Yes, sir."

"Very well. Make the selection yourself," and the waiter hurried away, still with the worried look on his face.

A man and woman entered the restaurant and walked straight to the table where Pamfret was sitting. They seemed surprised on seeing him seated there, looked around in a disconcerted manner, and finally sat down on a small divan placed against the wall. Pamfret thought he understood. He got up from his chair and bowed to the man.

"I beg your pardon, sir, but is this your table?"

The man nodded. "Yes—that is, we—we had it reserved," he answered.

"Well, then," said Pamfret, "I wouldn't think of appropriating it. The waiter should have told me. Of course you will take it?"

"But surely you know that would be against the law," exclaimed the other, horrified. "We couldn't."

"But that is exactly what I do not know," said Pamfret. "At least," he added, "I trust you will allow me to share it with you?"

The man looked at the woman inquiringly. She nodded. Pamfret found another chair, and all three sat down at the table together. The waiter appeared with a plate of soup, and seeming relieved to find the couple seated, took their order.

"I am surprised—" began the man.

"Of course you are," interrupted Pamfret. "But I really don't know the first thing about these beastly—these laws. The truth is—I have lived nearly all my life in China, where everything is different."

"But I thought the peace laws were universal."

"They are, they are," Pamfret replied hastily. "But I was alone most of the time—er—scientific explorations, you know. Besides they do this sort of thing better in China. There is no—"

"Rule 142. No comparisons," interrupted the woman.

There was silence for a while. Finally Pamfret tried again.

"Those broiled mushrooms were delicious," he declared. "Don't you think so?"

"I beg your pardon, but I'm afraid I can't answer you," replied the man. "Rule 207, you know. No contradictions."

Pamfret was becoming desperate. He had given his

head so many bumps against this immovable wall of
Peace that he was unable even to think. Silence, he decided, was his only refuge.

As the dessert came on he heaved a sigh of relief, and
foolishly ventured a question.

"You know," he said, "I have been out of the world for
a number of years, and I hope you won't mind if I ask
you a question. How long has this peace thing been in
power?"

"Really," answered the man, "you amaze me. Discussion of history is strictly forbidden."

Pamfret could stand it no longer. He threw a bill on the
table; took up his hat and stick and rushed wildly out of
the restaurant.

A car was passing the door. Pamfret ran to the next
corner ahead of it and waved his cane at the motorman.
The car went by without stopping, and as it passed the
conductor tossed a card out of the window. It fell on the
pavement at Pamfret's feet. He picked it up and read:

INTERNATIONAL PEACE CONGRESS.

COMMITTEE ON PUBLIC TRANSPORTATION.

Rule 96. The motorman or engineer of a public vehicle
shall ignore signals to stop for passengers, if such signals
are boisterous or agitated, or made in any but a thoroughly
peaceful manner.

Pamfret tore the card in a dozen pieces. "Well, of all
the—" he began, then he was silent. He was afraid to talk
even to himself where there was a chance of being overheard. He wanted to be alone, to have time to consider
this strange, this impossible world to which he had been
so eager to return. He started to walk downtown, intending to get a room in the first hotel he saw.

At Sixty-first Street he noticed a magnificent white mar-

ble building set back some fifty feet from the street, facing
Central Park. It was flanked by four minarets, each one
bearing at the top a marble group representing a winged
angel destroying a warrior's sword. Over the entrance, in
heavy raised letters, was the inscription HALL OF
PEACE.

"So this is where they do it," thought Pamfret, as he
gazed at the inscription. "I'd like to blow the d—d thing
up." Then he noticed that the main doors were open, and
passing over the outer flagstones with an odd feeling of
fear, he went inside.

The interior was very similar to that of a cathedral, with
the exception that there were no stained glass windows.
Immense columns of marble rose on every side, while the
vaulted roof seemed to reach to the skies. At the farther
end was an altar, on which was set the figure of the
winged angel destroying the warrior's sword. The group
was of ebony. Below, on the pedestal, were inscribed the
words of the Poet:

> "And therefore, to our weaker view,
> O'erlaid with black, staid Wisdom's hue,"

Around the altar rail below the figures men and women
were kneeling. Pamfret, as he gazed, felt a feeling of mingled disgust and awe sweep over him. "Of course," he
said to himself, "it is really very funny. But somehow it
impresses one." And he turned to leave.

A half-hour later found him seated in his room at the
Hotel Pax, reading a book. He had found it lying on the
table when he entered the room. It was covered in black
leather and lettered in gold with the title, "Book of Peace."
"By all the Gods!" exclaimed Pamfret. "Here's their bible!"

It was little more than a book of rules, with photographs
and biographies of the founders of the great Congress and
a short exposition of the philosophy of the new World

Religion. Everything, it seemed, was under the domination of this all-powerful Congress.

Pamfret, mentally disturbed as he was, found a great deal of amusement in the rules of the Committee on Courtship, while he found that the Committee on Domesticity had made the family a farce and the home a tomb. The Committee on Sleep—but Pamfret could go no further. He was completely exhausted. His head fell forward till his chin rested on his breast. Awakening with a start, he undressed and went to bed.

He dreamed of Peace, Peace with the body of an angel and a horrible grinning skull for a head. Through rivers and valleys, over steep hills and deep bogs and marshes this frightful thing pursued him, until at last he saw before him in the middle of a desert, the beautiful Hall of Peace. With a final burst of strength he reached the portal, and entering the marble vault, approached the altar and knelt before it. The ebony angel on the pedestal put together the pieces of the broken sword of the warrior, and raised it to strike. Pamfret raised his arm to ward off the blow; and just as the sword was descending with the speed of lightning, he awoke.

Someone was knocking on the door of his room. Pamfret, still shaking with the fear of his dream, called out, "Who is it?"

"In the name of the International Peace Congress and the Committee on Sleep, I ask that this door be opened," came a voice.

"What the devil have I done now?" thought Pamfret. "Disturbed the peace of my bedcovers, I suppose."

"In the name of the International Peace—" began the voice again.

"Oh, shut up!" said Pamfret under his breath, and crossed to the door and opened it. "What do you want?" he demanded.

The intruder eyed Pamfret serenely. He was dressed in white from head to foot, with a silver shield bearing the symbol of the angel and warrior on his breast. On his cap in gold letters was the word "Peace."

"What do you want?" Pamfret repeated.

"You were talking in your sleep," answered the Man in White. "Violation of Rule 34. Come."

"Come where?" asked Pamfret.

"You are pretending." But noting the blank look on Pamfret's face, he added, "To the Hospital for Talkers and Snorers."

"My God!" exclaimed Pamfret, and burst out laughing. "You don't mean to say that—"

"Ignorance is no excuse," the Man in White interrupted.

"But I have to dress."

"Well, I'll wait outside. You have five minutes."

Pamfret walked over to the chair by the window and sat down. He would have liked to have had time to think it all over, this grotesque, mad world that seemed to have lost its senses since he had left it sixty years before. As the scenes and events of the day passed through his mind he knew not whether to laugh or cry. Of course it was all very ludicrous, but—

"Time is up," called the Man in White through the door.

Pamfret crossed over to the closet where his coat was hanging and took from the inside pocket a small vial filled with a green liquid. Then he lay down on the bed and drank the liquid to the last drop. "Satan knew what he was about, after all," he murmured, and closed his eyes.

When the Man in White entered, the room was empty.

A COMPANION
OF FORTUNE

A rthur Churchill-Brown, attaché at the British Legation
in Rome, leaned back in his chair till it rested against
the rim of his desk, and squinted disagreeably at an open
letter which he held in his hand. This attitude of Arthur's
toward his desk was nothing unusual. According to his
unformed but practical philosophy, desks were made exactly for that purpose. He found a mild but never failing
interest in the almost constant stream of visitors who
passed down the narrow hall at the rear; and he thoroughly
abhorred the necessity of giving any attention whatever to
the papers and documents which were occasionally laid
behind him on his desk by the silent-footed attendant,
whose back, as he noiselessly returned to the inner rooms
of the secretary and the ambassador, seemed to Arthur to
suggest an almost intolerable insolence. Someday, he felt
sure, he would throw something at it.

On this particular morning the expression of bored an-
noyance which had come to be Arthur's official countenance had deepened to one of positive displeasure. "What

the deuce do they all come here for, anyway?" he
growled. "Good Lord! And they all go the same route.
It's enough to kill a man." He felt behind him on the desk
for a packet of cigarettes, lit one and, puffing furiously,
reread the offending letter. It ran as follows:

My Dear Son:

I have time for only a line, but I must get this off at
once. Miss Carlisle, a *very* wealthy American lady, and
her companion are leaving tonight for Rome. I met her
last month at Strathmore, and she has been staying with
me for a day or two in town. I have promised for you to
open some doors for her in Rome, and she will probably
call very shortly after you get this. Don't haul her out to
Udini's or any of the other places across the river.

Hastily,

Your loving Mother.

P.S.—I'll send you a check on the twentieth.

M. C. B.

Arthur sighed, wheeled his chair around and began to
wade through the pile of papers that had accumulated during his absence the day before. "She knows very well,"
he grumbled, "that I'm too busy to run all over the blooming town like a footman." Which was very true. Since his
promotion—he regarded the term as pure sarcasm—to the
Home Desk, he had been forced to spend at least an hour
of each day in real work. To a young diplomat who had
spent a full year in learning the delicate and subtle meth-
ods by which one may remain comfortably balanced between the Black and the White, this was indeed irksome.
It necessitated a complete readjustment. More than once
the picturesque inventions of a stranded beachcomber,
sent down from Naples by an overworked but still cred-
ulous consul, had violently disturbed the nice balance of
Arthur's social position in the Eternal City, where the

most alluring and entrancing eyes have a disconcerting
way of looking in two directions at once.

"Miss Carlisle," continued Arthur, still speaking aloud,
and emphasizing the title. "Of course, she's an old maid.
Probably forty, possibly fifty, and certainly plain. She'll
want to do the whole blooming round. If anybody had
asked me but——"

He was interrupted by the entrance of a servant, who
approached his desk and stood waiting for him to speak.

"Well?" said Arthur, without looking up.

"A lady, sir."

Arthur's worst fears were confirmed. As he advanced
to meet Miss Carlisle he swore, under his breath. Just in
the height of the season, to waste a week on this! She
could not be described better than in Arthur's own words:
probably forty, possibly fifty, and certainly plain. Lanky,
angular, and yet somehow graceful, she advanced to meet
the young diplomat with outstretched hand and a somewhat pleasing smile. Arthur extended his own hand, then
stood still, staring with rude frankness over Miss Carlisle's left shoulder.

"That," said the very wealthy American lady, "is just
what I expected. I've grown used to it in the past three
weeks. Miss Moulton," turning to the young woman who
had been the object of Arthur's surprised gaze, "this is
Mr. Churchill-Brown. Miss Moulton is my companion,"
she explained.

"Oh!" said the young man. Then, after a moment's silence, "O—Oh!" he repeated.

At which foolish remark no one would be surprised
who had ever had the good fortune to see Miss Moulton.
She was the exact antithesis of Miss Carlisle; and added
to the charm of her youth and beauty and loveliness was
a certain indefinable air of disdain that chained the young
man to the floor and left him speechless. While Miss Carlisle chattered amiably, something about having found
him absent when they called the day before, and did he

get her card, and wasn't Rome a wonderful place, and weren't the hotels the worst in the world, Arthur gazed openly at the companion, who finally found it necessary to turn away and begin an inspection of a portrait of the Duke of Wellington hanging nearby.

"But we don't want to bother you," Miss Carlisle finished breathlessly.

"Bother?" Arthur waved his hand in derision at the idea. "I have absolutely nothing to do." He felt a slight twinge of conscience as he glanced at the untouched pile on his desk; then his eye rested on the back of Miss Moulton, who was still inspecting the portrait. "Absolutely nothing," he repeated firmly. "I am only too delighted to be able to be of service to you. There is a luncheon today at the Guidi Palace—I'm sure you'll find it interesting. Then, this afternoon——"

"Today is full, I'm afraid—for us." Miss Moulton had turned to face them and was speaking in a coolly impersonal tone. "We are going to San Lorenzo, San Pietro and the Borghese. Really Mr. Churchill-Brown, there is no need to disturb you. But we are very grateful."

Arthur glanced at Miss Carlisle. "But I thought— Mother told me—" then at the amusement depicted on Miss Moulton's face he stopped short.

"I know," said the elder lady. "But what can I do?" She glanced at her companion and then turned helplessly to Arthur. "She tells me to go somewhere—and I go, whether I want to or not. What can I do?"

"Nothing whatever," the young man said gravely. "To tell the truth, I don't think you should object. When you can be piloted by one who—" Miss Moulton was regarding him suspiciously—"whose tastes lead to the Borghese—" Arthur grinned—"you should be more than satisfied. But I shall see you again?" He glanced appealingly at Miss Moulton who had started to leave. She turned at the door and looked at him for a moment over her shoulder.

"We are to be in Rome only a week," she said, hesitating. "Perhaps—we are staying at the Larossa." With a nod and a smile she tripped out, followed by Miss Carlisle, and through a window Arthur saw them enter a public brougham and drive away.

Now, there was nothing unusual in that, was there? Is there any more common sight in Europe than a pair of trippers calling at a legation? And do not all old maids have a companion? Are not these companions—especially in stories—always pretty? And yet—

Thirty minutes later Arthur muttered an impatient oath, sprang up from his chair and began walking up and down the room. "I'm a jolly idiot," he said firmly. "What do I care whether she snubbed me or not? Yet she told me her hotel—Well, what if she did? Who is she, anyway? A companion! I wonder—" he hesitated. "I *may* call on Miss Carlisle. She's a very dear lady. Very. Besides, it would please Mother. Mother evidently liked her. Moulton, eh? May be a cousin. May be a niece. I wonder if she—" he stopped short and stood for some minutes regarding the corner of his desk thoughtfully, then rang a bell, and when a servant appeared, ordered a carriage. Five minutes later he might have been overheard directing the driver, "To the Borghese."

If Lady Churchill-Brown, who was showing her daughter in as many places as possible during the short London season, had by some supernatural agency been enable to survey the movements of her son for the following two weeks, she would have been agreeably surprised and immensely pleased at the evident success of her plan to cure him of certain follies. Her treatment had consisted of an appointment to the diplomatic service. As though a young man who had been willing to misbehave in London would of necessity become an anchorite in Rome! Arthur had acted just as he might have been expected to act; in a very youthful and, maternally speaking, a thoroughly disgraceful manner.

Of this fact Lady Churchill-Brown was not entirely un-
aware; therefore would she have been highly gratified if
she had observed her son's actions for the two weeks following his meeting with Miss Carlisle—and her companion. He developed an incredible longing for moonlight
views of the Colosseum; he visited churches and villas
and galleries and ruins, gladly betraying his ignorance and
expressing humble gratitude for the instruction and en-
lightenment kindly furnished by Miss Moulton; he attended Miss Carlisle with unexampled assiduity and
devotion; he sat in corners at afternoon teas where they
talked in hushed tones of Gabriele d'Annunzio, or talked
of him not at all; and for fourteen whole days, never once
did he cross the bridge to Udini's! This last was in itself
a miracle.

Behold him then, on the morning following the expi-
ration of the two weeks, seated in a quiet and tastefully
furnished private parlor at the Hotel Larossa. In the centre
of the room was a pile of trunks and bags; Arthur was
sitting on one of the former. In a chair over by a window
was Miss Carlisle, wearing a dark blue traveling suit. She
was sitting bolt upright, with her hands resting on the arms
of her chair, evidently much disturbed by the startling
information just imparted to her by Arthur.

"It seems to me," she said, hesitating, "that you had
better speak to Miss Moulton."

There was a slight pause, while the young man twirled
his hat around in his hands nervously and gazed at the
door. Then he looked up at Miss Carlisle with an air of
determination. "It's this way," he said. "I may as well be
frank with you. I suppose I'll ask her anyway, but I want
to talk with you about it first. The fact is, I can't afford
it; though as far as I'm concerned it doesn't make the
slightest difference. It's only for her. What I want to know
is, who is she, and how long have you known her, and
all that sort of thing."

"Do you love her?"

"Yes."

"Well, then why don't you tell her so?"

Arthur was silent.

"Why don't you tell her?" Miss Carlisle repeated grimly.

"I—I'm afraid to," the young man stammered.

"Pooh!" the lady snorted contemptuously. "I can tell you one thing; you won't get any satisfaction out of me. Of course you're afraid! You're afraid she's poor. You're afraid her great-grandfather was as disrespectable as your own. And more than everything else, you're afraid of your mother!"

"I am not!" the young man declared hotly, his face very red.

"Yes you are!" Miss Carlisle almost shouted, rising and waving her arms excitedly. "Don't contradict *me!* And I can hardly blame you; She's worth a dozen of your kind. She's a thousand times too good for you. If she'd only had sense enough not to fall in love with you!"

"What!" cried Arthur, turning pale.

Miss Carlisle sank back into her chair. "Now what have I done?" she said helplessly. "Anyway, it was a lie. I wanted to see what you'd do."

"Oh!" said Arthur, doubtfully.

Then the door opened to admit Miss Moulton herself.

Arthur arose awkwardly, and there ensued the uncomfortable silence which always greets the entrance of one who has been the subject of conversation. The young lady looked from Arthur to Miss Carlisle and back again, as if to inquire the cause of their very evident embarrassment. Then the young man pulled two slips of blue paper from his pocket and advanced toward Miss Moulton with an attempt at naturalness that fell quite flat.

"Here are your tickets," said he, smiling foolishly. Miss Carlisle arose, muttered something unintelligible, and disappeared in the direction of her bedroom.

"What's the matter?" asked Miss Moulton coolly.

"Nothing," said Arthur, visibly ill at ease. "Nothing whatever. The fact is, I wanted to talk to you."

"Well?"

"Well—er—I—" he hesitated stammering.

"Go on," Miss Moulton said encouragingly.

Arthur gulped hard. "Haven't you noticed anything funny about me lately?" he demanded desperately.

"No—o, I think not. Are you ill?"

"Well, you see—" Arthur looked at her appealingly, "by Jove, I believe I am. The fact is, I—hang it all—I love you!"

"Indeed!"

"Yes, I do," he said doggedly, as though she had contradicted him. "Odd, isn't it?"

"Is it?" this with a rising inflection.

"Well, perhaps not exactly odd." He appeared to be considering the matter. "But very curious, you know—wonderful, and all that sort of thing. Er—moonlight rides, and all that sort of thing. I've thought of nothing else since I saw you. I'm a regular blooming idiot."

"Are you trying to make fun of me?"

The young man's face reddened and he straightened himself stiffly. "I am not," he declared, with dignity. "I am trying to ask you to marry me."

"Oh!" said Miss Moulton weakly. Evidently it was more than she had expected. She advanced a step toward Arthur, then turned aside and sat down in the chair recently vacated by Miss Carlisle. For a few seconds there was silence. Then,

"Of course," the girl sighed, "it's impossible."

"Oh, I say—"

"No," she interrupted firmly, "it is quite impossible. Quite. You know why as well as I do. But I—I really appreciate the honor you do me."

Arthur considered this for a minute in silence. Then he approached her chair and stood looking down at her un-

certainly. "Of course, I didn't think you loved me," he
said, his voice trembling. "But I thought there might be a
chance—and today you are leaving. It was just possible
that you cared for me a little—just enough to make it—
I say, you couldn't?"

Miss Moulton was silent.

"Because," Arthur went on, "if you do, nothing else
matters. Nothing about—you know what I mean. I know
I'm not rich. I know I'm a silly ass. I guess I never did
anything worthwhile in my life except fall in love with
you. I suppose I was a jolly fool to think you ever could
care for me."

A pause; then,

"I—didn't—say that." The voice was very low.

"Didn't say what?"

"That I couldn't—don't—care—for you."

Then, as he tried to look into her eyes, and as she res-
olutely kept them on the floor, "I say!" he begged, his
voice shrill and harsh with the ecstasy of hope, "look at
me!"

"I can't," she breathed faintly. "I can't—even—talk!"

Which was not very surprising, inasmuch as her face
was being held tightly against his shoulder with all the
strength of a lover's arms.

As a usual thing, this is where a story ends. The first
kiss is the last word. Both writer and reader seem to take
it for granted that as soon as a young man holds a girl in
his arms and tells her he loves her, that's all there is to
it. You, with your own experience to draw on for illus-
tration, may decide for yourself if the conclusion necessarily follows from so weak a premise.

In the present instance, whether or not Arthur
Churchill-Brown would really have married Miss Moulton, companion to the wealthy Miss Carlisle, may be
doubted, I think, without any extraordinary amount of
skepticism. The fact is, he didn't.

For to tell the truth, Arthur was by no means a hero. He was simply a very ordinary young Englishman, and despite his indignant denial of Miss Carlisle's keen accusation, he really was afraid of his mother.

On the evening following the ladies' departure from Rome, Arthur sat in his rooms on the Pidi, eating iced pineapple and gazing gloomily out of a window at the dimly lighted street. He and Miss Moulton were engaged to be married; there was no doubt that he loved her; and he had arranged to see her the following week at Venice. Yet he was unhappy. For somehow the vision which filled his thoughts was not the laughing, joyous face of his sweetheart, but that of Lady Churchill-Brown, filled with a consuming wrath. He pictured himself announcing calmly, "Mother, I am going to marry Miss Moulton, a young American girl. She is a traveling companion, and she is very poor, but I love her," and he shuddered, and admitted that such heroism was beyond him. He knew very well that the person whom he honored with the name of Churchill-Brown was expected to be such a one as could—and would—make a substantial addition to the woefully depleted Churchill-Brown coffers; the accomplishment of this purpose had become his mother's prime object in life. He was, indeed, between the devil and the deep sea.

And at that moment, hearing the door of his room open and close, he turned around in his chair.

Arthur sprang to his feet and advanced with outstretched hands. "Mother!" he cried. "What are you doing here? By Jove! I'm glad to see you." And he really was. For now, one way or another, the thing would soon be over.

"Humph!" grunted Lady Churchill-Brown, glancing around the room and finding a seat on a heavy divan, "I dare say you are. I came to see *you*. How does it happen you're at home?" she demanded, glaring at him as though his presence in his own rooms needed a thorough explanation.

Arthur's wits were sadly muddled. Energetic as Lady Churchill-Brown was, it was not her custom to make sudden and unexpected journeys from London to Rome. What had happened? Did she suspect something? Had Miss Carlisle written to her? Should he tell her, or not? And it must be admitted that somewhere in the back of his brain the young man had formed a grim resolution to stand by his guns and Miss Moulton to the very last. For whether he is a hero or not, it is always more or less dangerous to drive a man into a corner.

"Why, I—I had no place to go," said he. "Lucky, isn't it? Since you came."

"I don't know whether it's lucky or not. Where's Miss Carlisle?" his mother asked grimly.

"Gone to Venice. Didn't I write you?"

"Yes, you wrote me. When did she leave?"

"Today. They went on the afternoon express."

"Oh!" in a somewhat milder tone. Then, after a slight pause, and with a sigh of relief, "And how are you?"

"I'm all right," declared Arthur, with an attempt at lightness. "But why did you come?"

Lady Churchill-Brown considered for a minute. "To tell the truth," she said, "I had a shock. Now that the danger is past, it appears silly. In fact, I might have known better. I might have known you wouldn't do anything so ridiculous."

"Perhaps the danger isn't past." The words were out before Arthur realized what he was saying. He stood amazed at his own hardihood.

"What do you mean?" demanded his mother.

The young man took his courage between his teeth and held onto it firmly. Then he threw back his shoulders and directly faced the enemy. And then, at sight of the grim and aggressive face before him, his courage suddenly slipped down his throat and descended to the Lord knows where.

"I'm going to marry Miss Carlisle," he said.

"You are going to marry *who?*" shrieked his mother.

"Miss Carlisle," he repeated weakly. He had failed; at the crisis he had failed!

"Have you asked her?"

"Yes."

The effect of this announcement on Lady Churchill-Brown was startling. She sank back limply on the divan, clutching wildly at the air, while Arthur stared at her in amazement.

"What's the matter?" he demanded. "Isn't that what you've always wanted me to do?"

His mother, by a supreme effort of the will, lifted herself erect on the divan and sat regarding him in horrified silence. "Well, that ends it," she said finally. "My boy, you don't know what you've done. I suppose I deserved it. And I must admit it's not your fault."

Arthur was silent. Indeed, he hardly heard, being preoccupied with contemplating the hole into which he had just kicked himself.

"It was only yesterday morning I found it out," Lady Churchill-Brown went on presently. "Of course, you couldn't have known. Miss Carlisle isn't Miss Carlisle at all. She's Miss Moulton."

"What!" cried Arthur, springing to his feet.

"She's Miss Moulton," repeated his mother grimly, "and Miss Moulton is her. They did it because Miss Carlisle—the real Miss Carlisle—didn't want to be bothered by fortune-hunters. It's disgraceful. It's criminal. If I'd only known——"

"Do you mean to tell me"—Arthur was trying to remain calm—"that she—that Miss Moulton—that they—"

For a full minute he stood, allowing the meaning of this amazing information to sink into his befuddled brain.

Then a cherubic smile slowly illumined his face, and, seating himself on the divan, he took Lady Churchill-Brown's fat hand in his own and patted it rudely. "I say," he said happily, and thus started his sweet confession.

A WHITE PRECIPITATE

"Evans!"

"Yes, sir."

"Take these papers out of the room."

Without a sign of surprise at the unusual order, the servant gathered up the four morning newspapers and started to leave. As he reached the door he was again halted by his master's voice:

"And, Evans!"

"Yes, sir."

"If Mrs. Reynolds asks for them, tell her they haven't come."

"Yes, sir."

Left alone, Bernard Reynolds crossed to a chair by the open fire and seated himself thoughtfully. Even such a catastrophe as this of which he had just read failed to move him from his accustomed calm. Of course, the news must be told to his wife; how, was the difficulty. For himself, he was almost glad; materially inconvenient though it was, it meant the removal of a barrier which he had already found an impediment in his search for happiness. Further, he knew that Paula herself would find the immediate loss an ultimate benefit; but he also knew that, coming thus suddenly, the blow would be a hard one. It was with such methodical reflection that he met a shock which to most men would have meant keen disappointment, and to some despair.

As he extended his hand to lower the flame in the coffee-lamp. Evans reentered the room, bearing a loaded tray. Soon after, Paula came in. Bernard crossed the room to greet her, and escorted her to her chair at the table.

In the six months since the Reynoldses' wedding, the ceremony of breakfast had undergone a gradual but complete change. At the first dozen or so there had been very little eaten, and a great deal of foolishness. It had assumed the character of a morning worship, and Evans, who was orthodox, had been much disturbed by the order to place both chairs at one end of the table. At the present time, it was solely a matter of mastication and digestion. And yet Bernard declared—to himself—that the first had been by far the better, which seems to be a pretty good refutation of that disagreeable saying about men's stomachs.

On this particular morning the silence was oppressive. Even Evans seemed cast down by something unusual in the air, and was moved out of his habitual solemnity and dignity to an unheard-of sprightliness. When he served the jelly fifty seconds too soon, in a valiant attempt to start something, and received no notice whatever for his effort, he gave up in despair, and received his nod of dismissal with gratitude. When he had gone Paula raised her eyes from her plate for the first time and looked at Bernard. Her eyes were red, and her lips were set in a firm, straight line.

"I suppose," she said, "that last night settles it."

Bernard returned her gaze calmly. "What do you mean?"

"For six months we've been trying to decide whether

we've made a mistake. There is no longer any doubt about it."

Bernard hesitated a moment before replying "Paula, you've said something like this twice before. You know how I've tried—but it's useless. It's purely your imagination. You've discovered somehow that it's bad form to have dreams come true, and all I can do is to wait till you get over it."

"And last night—was that only my imagination?"

Bernard sighed hopelessly. "Will you never understand? Haven't I told you what my future demands?" Then, in a softer tone, "You know very well it's all for you. In order to succeed in my profession, a man must have friends. I'm trying to make them—that's all."

"And, I suppose, in order to be useful, they must be agreeable and—attractive."

"I've told you before that that's nonsense. It's pure rot. If you knew how silly——" He checked himself. "But I don't wish to be rude. There is a particular reason why I can't be. Only, for God's sake, have a little sense!"

For a full minute Paula was silent. The line of her mouth trembled, then tightened, and her hands, resting before her on the table, were clenched. Then, as though with an effort, she spoke slowly and calmly:

"Aren't you just a little tired of being a hypocrite, of living a lie?"

Bernard rose to his feet, astonished. "Paula!"

"That's what it amounts to. You may as well sit down and talk it over calmly. Ever since we were married, you've done nothing but lie and pretend."

"Paula! For God's sake——"

"Please *listen*. I'm not going to descend to heroics, and I don't care to listen to any. We may as well face the truth. We made a bad bargain, but we may as well admit it *was* a bargain. You pretend to love me, and I"—she caught her breath, and then went on calmly—"I pretended to love you. I don't know why I did it, but I know why you did. Of course, you wanted my money. As for me, I suppose it was your talent, your career."

Bernard, still sitting opposite her, controlled his voice with an effort. "You seem to have analyzed us thoroughly," he said dryly. "And you—you are sure it was only pretense?"

"Have I not said so?" Paula laughed harshly. "Of course, it hurts your vanity. But you'll soon get over it. Besides, it will restore your peace of mind. You will no longer be under the necessity of attempting to deceive me. Our marriage becomes purely a business partnership, to which you furnish the brains and I the money. There will be no more nonsense about an affection that doesn't exist."

"Paula, I don't believe you." The voice was strained, appealing. "Whatever you may think of me, I can't believe you to be—as you say you are. I *won't!*"

"I have said——" Paula began coldly.

"I know." There was a sudden change in Bernard's voice. "And it would hardly be a compliment to suppose you are lying *now*. Very well; I accept your terms. It is strictly a business partnership. You admit I have the brains?"

"Of course."

"And you the money?"

"That is what I said."

"And the one, I believe, balances the other?"

"What is the use of repeating it all?" Paula's voice held both weariness and despair.

"I just want to get it straight. I want to know exactly where I stand. You are sure I am furnishing my full share?"

"What do you mean?" cried Paula, startled by his tone.

Bernard, ignoring her question, struck the bell on the table sharply, and when Evans appeared, almost immediately, turned to him.

"Bring me the *Morning News*."

Evans disappeared, and a minute later returned with one of the newspapers which he had previously been told to remove. Bernard, his hand slightly trembling, handed it across the table to Paula, indicating with his finger a double-column head on the first page. His voice was tense with feeling as he said:

"That is what I mean."

As her eyes caught the headline Paula gave a little involuntary cry, and the paper fell from her hands. Then, as she read the first two or three paragraphs, and realized the full meaning of them, her face grew pale and her eyes sought Bernard's in a sort of dumb protest.

"It isn't true!" she cried.

Bernard was silent.

"It *can't* be true! It means—everything is gone! It can't be true!"

Then, while Bernard sat silently regarding her, she bent over the paper and read the article through to the end. When she spoke her voice was dry and hard. "If—but there are no ifs. It is all gone. I have nothing. I am a pauper."

"Worse than that." Bernard spoke grimly. "You are in debt. I spoke to Grimshaw an hour ago over the telephone. Dudley has disappeared—which means that his liabilities must be met by you. Grimshaw says there is absolutely no hope."

Paula stared at him as though fascinated, unable to speak.

"Well?" she said finally.

Bernard arose and, passing around the table, stood by her chair. "It *is* well," he said, looking down at her. "Our partnership is dissolved."

Paula recoiled as though he had struck her. "You mean——"

"What I say. And I thank God for it! Do you think I haven't known what you've been thinking all these months? A thousand times I have read in your eyes all—

and more—that you have said this morning. It has made
my life unbearable. That is why I'm glad it's all over—
that the weary farce is ended."

"Then—you are through?"

"With the partnership, yes. Your share of the capital
has disappeared; therefore the firm belongs to me. My first
care will be to keep it intact." He stood silent for a moment, regarding her gravely.

"It isn't what you said that hurts. Your every action and
thought has been a silent accusation which it was impossible for me to answer. I have been dumb, but not blind.
You have condemned me without a hearing. You needn't
have told me that you have never loved me; if you had,
you could never have believed me to be—what you have
said."

Paula lifted her eyes slowly, and tried in vain to meet
his. Then, suddenly, the strength of her lie failed her; she
buried her face in her hands and sobbed brokenly. "I can't
give you up! I *can't!*" she moaned.

Then, as though by magic, Bernard's face cleared, and
was filled with light. "Good God! Of course not!" he exclaimed fiercely. "I won't let you! Didn't I say the firm
belongs to me?"

When Evans answered the bell, ten minutes later, he
stopped short in the doorway and viewed the scene before
him with unconcealed dismay. Both chairs—occupied—
were placed squarely together at the farther end of the
table.

"Evans," said Bernard, "I want to ask you a question.
I suppose you have read the papers?"

"Yes, sir."

"Then, you know of our—good fortune. Thank God,
we have to economize! Your—er—pickings will probably
be reduced. The question is, do you want to stay?"

"No, sir," said Evans promptly. "Not if I have to serve
breakfast. I can stand the rest."

"Evans!"

"How can I help it, sir? Look at that!" He pointed at the chairs indignantly. "You know, sir, I've always tried to keep my self-respect, which I can't do going into rooms *backwards*. And even for the sake of your father——"

"Very well." Bernard grinned happily. "We'll have Maggie serve breakfast after today."

Evans turned to go.

"But," Bernard continued, "this morning you'll have to suffer. Bring back the fruit tray and make another pot of coffee. We're going to celebrate."

THE MOTHER OF
INVENTION

🎵

William Frederick Marston blew a cone of cigarette smoke thoughtfully into the air, sighed despairingly, and read the cablegram for the third time:

WALK HOME TIRED OF YOUR FOOLISHNESS NOT A
CENT.   *Jonathan Marston.*

"I suppose," said William Frederick aloud, "he thinks he's funny. And the first two words, which are entirely useless and perfectly offensive, cost him an extra half-dollar. The governor is getting extravagant."

He tossed his cigarette into a porcelain urn on the table, lit another, and crossing the room, seated himself in a chair by the window and gazed thoughtfully out at the throng in the street below.

The hour was half past three in the afternoon; the street, the Rue Royale, Paris. Trim speedy taxicabs, with their air of fussy importance, glided along the farther curb; here and there an old-fashioned cabriolet or hansom dodged helplessly about in the rush of the modern traffic. The pedestrians sauntered, strolled, trotted, paraded—did everything, in short, except walk. The chauffeurs and cab drivers courteously exchanged scurrilous epithets, the *sergent de ville* at the corner blew his whistle furiously, waving his arms wildly in all directions, and barefooted gamins darted through the crowd, crying late evening editions of the newspapers. Over all was the soft radiance of the September sun.

But the humor and color of this animated scene was entirely lost upon William Frederick Marston. Perched high in the air on the horns of a dire dilemma, he was madly struggling in a desperate effort to regain a footing on solid earth.

For perhaps half an hour he remained sitting by the window, smoking many cigarettes and trying to think. But his situation was so fantastically horrible, so utterly unprecedented, that he found it impossible to shape his thoughts. There was no ground on which to build. The hypothesis being absurd, how could he be expected to arrive at a logical conclusion?

Suddenly he rose to his feet, thrust his hand into his vest pocket and drew forth three franc-pieces and one or two sous. For a moment he gazed at them mournfully, then returned them to his pocket, crossed to a wardrobe, took from it his hat and gloves, and left the room.

In fifteen minutes he returned, looking, if possible, more dejected than before. He entered the room with a slow, irresolute step, closing the door behind him with exaggerated care. Depositing his hat and gloves on the table, he crossed the room and stood by the window. Again he thrust his hand into his vest pocket, and drew it forth. It contained three sous. Opening the window, he tossed them into the street below and smiled with tragic amusement as he saw three or four gamins dart toward them. Then, with a deep sounding sigh, he sank back in a chair by the window, muttering, "I—Billy Marston—to lose *three francs* at roulette! It is horrible."

It was, indeed; too, it was incredible. But alas! It was true. And now the three francs were gone, and William Frederick Marston began to think in earnest.

How it had come about he could scarcely have told. His recollection of the events of the three months previous was somewhat dimmed by their whirlwind rapidity and unusual and varied character. He had a faint memory of an affair of the heart *à la* Byron at Milan, a disgraceful though amusing experience among the beachcombers at Marseilles, and a disastrous hour of recklessness at Monte Carlo. He had mentioned none of these incidents in his letters to his father, Jonathan Marston, of New York, who had seen fit to send his son, William Frederick, on an educational tour of the Mediterranean during the summer vacation preceding his senior year at Harvard.

The tour of the Mediterranean had been abruptly halted by the misfortune at Monte Carlo. William Frederick had cabled to New York for additional funds and on receiving them he had departed for Paris. Struck by the beauty of that city, he had immediately decided to buy it, and discovered too late that he had squandered his last sou on a worthless option. The fall term at Harvard was to begin in two weeks. He cabled his father:

LEAVE FOR NEW YORK TOMORROW WIRE FUNDS.
                                        William.

That cablegram promptly brought the following answer:

FIVE HUNDRED MORE YOU NEED A GUARDIAN.
                                        Father.

But by that time the lure of the City by the Seine had William Frederick in its deadly grasp. Three days later he sent another cablegram:

FUNDS DISAPPEARED WIRE QUICK SAIL TO-
MORROW.   *William.*

In a few hours came the following answer:

PASSAGE ON *Alvonia* SAILING CHERBOURG TENTH
PAID HERE AM SENDING TWENTY DOLLARS FOR FARE
TO CHERBOURG.   *Father.*

William Frederick, commenting indignantly on the folly and immorality of suspicious parents, obtained the twenty dollars and purchased a ticket for Cherbourg, whither he decided to betake himself the following morning. The ticket, however, was but thirty francs. That evening he entered a certain gay and noisy apartment in the Montparnasse Quarter with fifty francs in his pocket, and came out with two thousand. On the following day, at the hour the *Alvonia* sailed from Cherbourg, he was walking in the Champs Elysées, ogling aristocratic carriages and trying to decide whether to spend the evening on the Mountain or at the Folies Bergère.

Three days later he sent the following cablegram, collect:

MISSED STEAMER WIRE FUNDS OR ARRANGE TRANS-
PORTATION.   *William.*

And it was in answer to this that he had received the unfeeling and sarcastic advice from his father to walk home. And William Frederick, being a wise son and therefore knowing his own father, was very well aware of the fact that what Jonathan Marston said, he meant.

He was, in fact, tired of Paris. He wanted to go home.

The governor must know that. And the fall term at the
university would commence in three days. He felt a sudden fierce yearning for knowledge. Was his father so unfeeling as to deny him the advantages of a decent
education? Did he not realize the imperative necessity for
one's attendance at one's preliminary lectures and reci-
tations? Surely he must. Another cablegram would persuade him.

But no. Pride had something to say about that. Since
his father had seen fit to refuse his reasonable request for
money to come home, he would make no further appeal
to *him*. Such an appeal, he told himself bitterly, would be
useless anyway. Some other expedient must be found.

He had friends, of course—dozens of them. There were
one or two whom he could trust utterly—Sackville Du
Mont, for instance, or Tom Driscoll, of Philadelphia. But
they, poor devils, could be of no use in a financial difficulty. And the others would talk. That would serve his
father right—to have it known all over New York that the
son of Jonathan Marston had been forced to depend on
the assistance of friends to get home when an unforeseen
shortage of funds had overtaken him during his travels in
Europe. If his father showed no concern for the dignity
of the Marston name, why should *he*?

But here, again, entered pride. And the pride of youth,
when properly nourished and aroused, is capable of magnificent sacrifices and supreme idiocies. It caused William
Frederick to reject with scorn the idea of an appeal for
money to his acquaintances; it caused him to regard the
conduct of his father with increasing indignation and resentment; it caused him, finally, to resolve grandly that he
would make his way home unaided and alone. Sublime
resolution!

He proceeded immediately to the consideration of ways
and means. The obvious and ordinary method he dismissed with contempt. It was all very well for common
persons to peel potatoes or feed cattle for a passage across

the Atlantic—indeed, Tom Driscoll had done it, and he thought none the less of him for it—but such a degradation could not even be thought of in the case of William Frederick Marston. It was a sheer impossibility. In fact, he regarded as absolutely necessary the luxuries and privileges of the first cabin. This greatly increased the difficulty of an otherwise simple task. He must use his wits.

He used them. A thousand schemes offered themselves to his mind, each to be rejected in its turn. As for earning the money for a passage, that was impossible. He had no ability that was marketable, even in that greatest and most varied of all markets—Paris. He realized it with a sense of amazement.

But there must be a way. He enlarged his scope of speculation. Stowaway? Bah! Take passage on a liner, pretend to have lost his ticket, and trust to Fortune and the name of Marston? But that would mean an appeal to his father, perhaps even a demand on him by the steamship company. Besides, there was the fare to Cherbourg, and incidentals. Appeal to Ambassador Halleck? But that, again, would mean an appeal to his father, though indirectly.

If he only possessed Tom Driscoll's experience and daring! Tom could do anything—and would. And was not he the equal of Tom Driscoll? Ha! His pride rose higher and higher, carrying William Frederick with it in ever-widening circles, until finally he arrived in the realm of pure artistic creation. Here the question of morality ceases to exist. The intellect, freed from the troublesome problems of ethics and legality, conceives, with a sole and single aim, the satisfaction of its own desires.

And then, suddenly, the face of the young man was illumined with a great light. This gave place to a deep, painful frown; and the frown, in its turn, to a sublime and portentous grin. He crossed to the table for a cigarette and finding the box empty, fished one of his discarded stubs from the procelain urn and lit it with the detached air of a genius at his easel.

"After all," he muttered, "I shall have to ask Tom to help, but not with money. The question is, will he do it? Well—he *must*. I'll make it as strong as I can. And—let's see—there's the William Penn Tablet, and the Thomas Jefferson Memorial, and the Statue of Franklin, and the Old Tower—"

William Frederick Marston had achieved an immortal conception.

At this point this tale assumes the dignity and importance of history, and we shall let the chroniclers speak for themselves. From the *Philadelphia Clarion*, September 21:

LIBERTY BELL DEFACED
Name of French Palmist Appears
in Red Paint on its Surface

Police are at a Loss to Discover Perpetrator of Deed of Vandalism and are in Communication with the State Department at Washington.

Late last evening, or early this morning, some person or persons entered Independence Hall by a window at the rear and defaced the Liberty Bell by painting on it, in large red letters, the following:

Jules Mercade
Chiromancien
37 Rue de Rennes
Paris

The outrage was first discovered by H. P. Sawyer, who entered the room at eight o'clock this morning to assume his duties as guardian of the bell. He first noticed that the window leading from the room to the park at the rear was open. Startled, he hurried to the Bell to assure himself of its safety and soundness, and found it disfigured in the manner described above.

The guard whose duty it was to close up the building last night declares that the window was locked by him at nine o'clock; but that question is really of no importance, since the fastening was old and rusty, and could have been easily forced even without the aid of a tool. No one can be found who saw any person either in the park at the rear or near the window. The vandal evidently chose an hour when he was certain to be unobserved. The police have been unable to discover any clue whatever to his whereabouts or identity.

The authorities are at a loss to account for any possible motive. There was no attempt, apparently, at permanent mutilation. The paint used was ordinary house paint, easily removable by the application of turpentine. If it is really, as it seems to be, an advertisement of a French palmister who expects to escape punishment for the outrage he has instigated because of his distant residence from the scene of its commission, Monsieur Mercade will quickly discover his mistake. The State Department has already communicated with the proper authorities at Paris, asking them to apprehend Mercade, and a reply is expected not later than this afternoon.

This deplorable affair has revealed the lamentable lack of proper care by the authorities of our public museums and historical relics. It may be asserted without fear of successful contradiction ....

September 22nd:

It will be a matter of pleasure and gratification to learn that Jules Mercade, whose name was found painted on the Liberty Bell yesterday morning, was arrested at his rooms at 37 Rue de Rennes, Paris, early yesterday afternoon.

According to Paris dispatches, Mercade exhibited no surprise at his arrest, since which time he has preserved a profound silence. He has even refused to admit his identity, and the police have been unable to establish it, since he appears to have occupied the rooms at 37 Rue de Rennes for only few days before his arrest. The prisoner seems, indeed, to be much amused at the position in which he finds himself, and it is the opinion of the French authorities that he expects to escape punishment for his act on account of lack of evidence, and then reap the advantage of the publicity his name has received.

Mercade has agreed to dispense with the formality of extradition on condition that he receive first-class steamship accommodations and that there be no outward sign of his status as a prisoner; and to this peculiar bargain the French authorities have agreed at the request of Ambassador Halleck, in order to avoid delay.

He will sail tomorrow from Cherbourg, on the *Daconia*, accompanied by a member of the Paris police.

September 29th:

If there be such a person as "Jules Mercade," and if he be responsible for the defacement of the Liberty Bell on September 21, it seems likely that, owing to the bungling of the Paris police, he will go unpunished.

The "Jules Mercade" whom a police officer brought over on the *Daconia*, which arrived at New York yesterday, proved to be no less a personage than William Frederick Marston, son of Jonathan Marston, the New York financier.

Young Marston seems to

regard his experience as an amusing escapade, and though he is unable, or unwilling, to explain how he came to be taken for "Jules Mercade," and indeed refuses to discuss the affair in any way whatever, it is evident that he has enjoyed himself immensely at the expense of the much-vaunted Paris police. He was, of course, immediately released.

But Mr. Marston, however much he has enjoyed himself, has aided in the defeat of the ends of justice—though without such intention—by failing to assert and prove his identity at the time of his arrest. No doubt, he had gotten a great deal of fun out of it. But the defacement of the Liberty Bell was an offense against national sentiment and dignity, and all good citizens will agree that . . .

At about eight o'clock in the evening of the day on which the *Daconia* arrived in New York, two men were seated, smoking at the dinner table in the Marston home on Fifth Avenue. The ladies had departed about fifteen minutes previously. The elder man was puffing thoughtfully on a large black Cazadores; the younger had consumed two cigarettes and was starting on a third.

"That bridge over the Tiber at Athens is wonderful," said the younger man suddenly, breaking the oppressive silence with an effort. "I don't wonder you insisted I shouldn't miss it." He chattered on for a minute, stammered, and stopped.

"William," said the elder man in a voice deep, well modulated, and musical, "You're a perfect ass. Don't try to play the innocent baby with me. I know you too well. At the same time, I have made a discovery. There is one man in this world who is even a bigger idiot than you are."

Judging by the calm tranquility with which the younger man received these rather forceful phrases, it is to be supposed that he had heard them before. He poured himself a pony of cognac and passed it to and fro under his nose.

"Of course," he said, sniffing with appreciation, "you arouse my curiosity. Who may this inconceivable idiot be?"

The elder man drew in a mouthful of smoke and expelled it with the proper care and deliberation before he answered. "The man," he said, "who, at your request, painted a monstrous, red, hideous sign on the Liberty Bell of our great country." Jonathan Marston, the terrible, smiled reminiscently—a smile of wisdom and understanding.

"And by the way," he continued presently, "it is really too bad that your little plot made it necessary to change your address. Of course that was why you missed my last cablegram. My advice to walk home was meant merely as a temporary pill. I wired you five hundred dollars the following day."

MÉTHODE AMÉRICAINE

Pierre Dumian sat at a table in the Café Sigognac, sipping a glass of vichy and reading an article in *L'Avenir*. From time to time he gave an impatient grunt, which occasionally reached an audible ejaculation as his eye met a phrase particularly displeasing. Finally he tossed the paper onto the chair at his side and, placing his elbows on the table and his chin in his hands, gazed steadily at his empty glass with an air of deep disgust.

Pierre never felt very well in the morning. True to his calling, he was always more or less uneasy in the sunlight; besides, one must pay for one's indiscretions. But on this particular morning he was more than uncomfortable: he was in genuine distress. He was pondering over a real misfortune. What an ass he had been! Surely he had been insane. Nothing less could account for it. He cast a glance at the newspaper, extended his hand toward it, then nervously resumed his former position. The thing was absurd—absolutely absurd. How could it have been taken seriously? He would write an apology—a correction. But

no, that was no longer possible. Decidedly, he must see
it through; there was his reputation. Well, for the future
he would be careful—very careful. He would be more
than circumspect: he would be absolutely polite. But—
Bah! What a horrible thought! Perhaps there would be no
future? Perhaps this would be his last? This was too much
for Pierre's excited nerves. He straightened himself in his
chair, muttered an oath half-aloud, and called to a waiter
for another glass of vichy. It was at this moment that he
felt a hand on his shoulder and heard a voice at his side.
Turning, he beheld Bernstein, of *Le Matin*.

"Ah! I congratulate you, my friend," he was saying.

Pierre was on his guard instantly. So the story had already gotten around! Clearly, there was no way out of it.
With an effort he forced an easy smile, glanced meaningly
around the half-filled room, and with a gesture invited the
newcomer to be seated.

Bernstein, noticing the glass which the waiter was placing before Pierre, elevated his brows and shrugged his
shoulders. "Nerves?" he inquired pleasantly.

Pierre resented the implication, mainly because it was
true. He grunted a negative, lifted the glass and drained
its contents, then spoke in a tone of indifference.

"It is necessary to take care of myself. I expect to
need—but perhaps you don't know. Why did you congratulate me?"

Bernstein winked slyly. "Ah! But, my friend, it is useless. The whole world knows it. Over at Lampourde's they
are already laying wagers, and at the office the talk is of
nothing else. They all envy you. Or, at least, they would
envy you if—" Bernstein hesitated and looked at Pierre
curiously.

"Well?" said Pierre, with an attempt at lightness. "If—"

"Nothing," said the other quickly. "For, as to that, life
itself is a gamble. We must take our chances. And what
courage! What glory! What fame! Why, my friend, on the

day after tomorrow you can go to old Lispenard and say to him: 'Henceforth I shall expect a thousand francs each for my signed articles.' And what can he do? That is, of course, if you can go to him at all."

Pierre laughed contemptuously. "I'm not so easily frightened, if that's what you mean. What of that?" he picked up the newspaper on the chair at his side and tossed it across the table.

Bernstein glanced at it and nodded. "Of course," he agreed, "it is admirable, wonderful. All the same, you were a fool. You should not have allowed him to choose. This fellow Lamon is dangerous."

To this Pierre replied with a contemptuous snap of the fingers. The other continued:

"No, but he is. You understand, my friend, it is only for your own good I tell you this. I had it from someone at Lampourde's, I don't remember whom. This Lamon is dangerous."

There was something in the tone that caused Pierre's hand to tremble as he extended it toward his glass.

"You know," Bernstein went on, "he came here but a month ago from Munich. This play was written there. He was stationed there as an officer in a German regiment. And his reputation in affairs similar to yours was such that they called him '*Lamon, le diable.*' That is why I say you have made a mistake. For with the rapier you might get a scratch—no more."

Pierre, during this recital, was doing his best to appear unconcerned. But the pallor of his face was painfully evident and his voice was husky as he said:

"Who told you this?"

"I have forgotten. But, after all, what does it signify? A little practice today and tomorrow, a little luck—and you will be the most talked-of man in Paris. I tell you, you are to be envied; always provided—I speak frankly, my friend—always provided that Lamon misses."

Pierre shuddered. He began to hate Bernstein. What did

he mean by this horrible calmness, this brutality? It was certainly a lie, this story about Lamon. Assuredly it was impossible; otherwise, he would have heard it before. Thus, with his brain whirling madly, he sat and pretended to listen to Bernstein, who rattled on endlessly about Lamon, the gossip of the boulevards, the latest news of the profession. Pierre heard not a word; and a half-hour later, when Bernstein was called away by an appointment, he breathed a sigh of relief and quickly made his way to the street.

Someone has said, somewhere, that there are times when it is braver to run than to fight. Let us hope, for Pierre's sake, that the present instance was a case in point; for he had decided to run. He admitted this at once—to himself—without reservation or shame, standing in front of the Sigognac, staring with unseeing eyes at the passing throng of vehicles. Bernstein's story of Lamon's prowess had finished him utterly and instantly.

The question was: would it be possible to do the thing gracefully? For Pierre loved his skin only just a little better than his reputation, and he ardently desired to save both of them. His brow contracted in a worried frown; he shrugged his shoulders; he sighed. That devil of a Lamon! But now that he had finally decided in favor of his skin, Pierre felt much easier; and soon he devoted his mind entirely to devising a means of escape. An apology was clearly out of the question; he would be laughed at from one end of Paris to the other; and what was more to the point, that demon Lamon would most probably not accept it. A hundred schemes presented themselves and were in turn rejected, and Pierre was ready to give way to despair. There seemed to be nothing for it but ignominious flight. Then suddenly his eyes flashed with joy—an idea! He considered—it was perfect! He turned and started off down the street at a pace calculated to land him in the Seine within five minutes. Then, recollecting himself, he halted and waved his arms wildly at the driver of a cab across the street. A minute later he was rolling rapidly along in the direction of the Montparnasse Quarter.

It was in front of a shabby, dilapidated building in the Rue de Rennes that the cab finally stopped. Pierre instructed the driver to wait, glanced doubtfully around, looked again at the number over the door, and finally ventured within. At the end of a hall on the first floor he found a door bearing the inscription:

ALBERT PHILLIPS
Professeur d'Escrime
Méthode Américaine

Pierre, entering in response to the "Come in," which greeted his knock, found himself in a long, low, bare apartment, only less dingy than the hall which led to it. On a chair near the door lay some fencing foils, two or three pairs of boxing gloves, and a dilapidated mesh mask. The only other chair in the room, placed in front of a table over near the single window, was occupied by a shabby-looking individual who turned his head at a slight angle as his visitor entered. Pierre, whose eyes were still unaccustomed to the dim light, stood blinking uncertainly. The man at the table turned slowly around and faced him.

"I have come," said Pierre, "to arrange a matter of business. But I believe you are not the right man."

"Then why did you come?"

"Would you care to earn a thousand francs?" asked Pierre after a moment's reflection.

Monsieur Phillips betrayed his first sign of interest. "My dear sir," he replied, "there are very few things in this world I would not undertake for a thousand francs."

"That is well," said Pierre. "But before we proceed further, can you shoot—with the pistol?"

The other frowned and glanced up quickly. "Better than anyone else in Paris," he announced. "But I have said that there are a few—"

"It is an affair of honor," Pierre interrupted.

Phillips elevated his brows. "That's different. Go on."

Still Pierre hesitated. Then, with a gesture of decision he crossed to the chair near the door, rolled off its encumbrances onto the floor, and placing it by Phillips's table, seated himself.

"Of course," he began, "you can keep a secret?"

"For a thousand francs—yes."

"That is well. You shall be paid. What I want is easily told. I am challenged to a duel with pistols at twenty paces on Thursday morning at six o'clock. I want—I want you to take my place."

Phillips gave a start of surprise and looked keenly at Pierre. "It is impossible," he said finally. "I should be detected."

"That is my risk. Besides, I can arrange it perfectly. Do you accept or not?"

"Where is the duel to be fought?"

"On the bank of the Seine, just south of the Pont de Suresnes."

"That's dangerous. For you must know the new prefect has issued an edict—"

"That also can be arranged," Pierre interrupted.

"Well—who is your man?"

"Lamon, the dramatist."

"Ah!" Phillips hesitated and appeared to be lost in thought, while his lips were compressed in a curious smile. "I accept," he said finally.

"Good!" Pierre breathed a sigh of relief. "Then there remain only the details."

"Which are somewhat important," the other observed dryly. "Proceed, monsieur."

Pierre hitched his chair a little nearer and continued: "First, there is the matter of identity. Well, you are nearly of my size; you will wear my clothing, and you will go masked."

"How can you arrange that?"

Pierre brushed aside the objection with a wave of the hand. "Very simple. You spoke of the edict of the new prefect of police. I shall insist that we wear masks in order to avoid recognition. I shall also arrange to go to the rendezvous alone—any pretext will serve. All you need do is to be there at the appointed hour, speak little and— shoot straight."

"And who are you?"

"You do not know me?" Pierre asked in a tone of surprise.

"I know no one."

"Dramatic critic on *L'Avenir*," said Pierre, taking a card from his case and handing it to the other.

"Ah! This, then, is professional?"

"Yes. I have never even seen Lamon ... Of course there are other details to be arranged, and it will be safest for you to wear one of my suits. I will bring it myself tomorrow morning." Pierre was moving toward the door.

Phillips rose from his chair. "But, monsieur! The thousand francs."

"I will bring you five hundred tomorrow morning; the remainder after the duel."

For that afternoon and evening and the following day, Pierre found much work to do. The arrangement of details proved to be not so simple as he had expected. The seconds of Monsieur Lamon fell in readily with his scheme of masking; but Pierre's own friends were not so easily persuaded. They denounced it as childish and absurd, inasmuch as the projected duel was an open topic of discussion in every café in Paris; and they particularly objected to their principal's determination to go to the rendezvous unattended. The thing was unprecedented, monstrously irregular; it would amount, on their part, to an absolute breach of duty. "Our honor, our very honor, will be compromised! It is impossible!" But Pierre, who had much more than honor at stake, prevailed against all entreaties and protests.

On Wednesday morning he spent a full hour in Phillips's room, coaching him against every possible mischance. Luckily Phillips was acquainted with the appearance of one of his seconds, and Pierre gave him a minute description of the other; and since Pierre himself had never seen Lamon, Phillips would of course not be expected to recognize him. As to any minor oddities of gesture or voice they would be easily accounted for as the result of the strain under which the duelist might be supposed to labor. Pierre finally rose from his chair with a gesture of approbation.

"Perfect!" he declared, surveying Phillips from head to foot. "I wouldn't know the difference myself." Opening a purse, he took from it five hundred-franc notes and laid them on the table. "There is half. And remember, this is the most important of all: after it is over, come at once to the Restaurant de la Tour d'Ivoire. There you will change your garments and become Monsieur Phillips again, and I will pay the remainder. It will be difficult, for they will insist on accompanying you, but you must manage it somehow."

Phillips picked up the banknotes, folded them and placed them in his pocket. Then, turning to Pierre, "There is one thing we have not considered," he said. "What if I am wounded?

Then the fraud would be discovered."

Pierre's face paled. "I had thought of that. But we must take our chances. And you—for God's sake, shoot first, and shoot straight."

"Monsieur Dumain," said Phillips, "rest easy. When I aim at this Lamon, I shall hit him."

But that night Pierre was unable to sleep. Whenever he closed his eyes he found himself looking into the muzzle of a revolver which, in size, bore a strong resemblance to a cannon. This was disquieting. Pierre sat up in bed and reached for a cigarette. "It's absurd," he said aloud. "I'm as shaky as though I were going to do it myself."

At half-past four he rose, dressed, and finding the cab he had ordered at the door, proceeded through the silent, dim streets toward the Pont de Suresnes.

The rear of the Restaurant de la Tour d'Ivoire, which Pierre had selected as his place of retreat during the duel, overlooked the Seine at a point about a hundred yards up the river from this bridge. It was dilapidated, shabby, and disrespectable; which was exactly what Pierre desired. What with a garrulous *concierge* and a prying neighborhood, to have remained in his own rooms would have been hazardous; and the Restaurant de la Tour D'Ivoire, besides the advantages already named, possessed the further and greatest one of an old window with broken panes which looked out directly upon the scene of the duel.

The clock was hard on five as Pierre entered the restaurant and accosted the proprietor, who was dozing in a lump behind the little wooden desk. He awoke with a start and looked angrily at the intruder.

"What do you want?" he demanded.

"I desire a private dining room," said Pierre.

The greasy old man looked angrier still. "The devil you do!" he shouted. "There isn't any." He settled back into his chair and immediately fell asleep. Pierre shrugged his shoulders, glanced around, and noticing a door in the opposite corner, passed through it into the room beyond.

This room was cold, dirty and filled with that particularly disagreeable odor which is the effect of stale tobacco smoke and poisoned breaths in a close atmosphere. Tables and chairs were piled in confusion at one end; a row of them extended along the farther wall; and the only light was that which came in through the window with broken panes overlooking the Pont de Surenes entrance, and its fellow directly opposite. Three or four men, sleeping with their heads nodding at various angles, were scattered here and there on the wooden chairs; another was seated at a table with a bottle before him reading a newspaper; and a drowsy and bedraggled waiter rose to his feet and stood blinking foolishly as Pierre entered.

Pierre, having seated himself and ordered a bottle of wine, looked up to meet the curious gaze of the man with the newspaper. It was sustained almost to the point of impertinence, and at once made Pierre uneasy. Was it possible he had been recognized? The fellow's dress was very different from that of the ordinary habitué of holes such as the Restaurant de la Tour d'Ivoire; and though Pierre could find nothing familiar in either the face or figure, he became every minute more restless and suspicious; until, finally, he accosted the stranger.

"It is very cold," he said, in as indifferent a tone as possible, glancing up at the broken window through which the damp river air found its way.

The stranger started and glanced up quickly. "Were you speaking to me, monsieur?"

"I did myself that honor," said Pierre.

"And you said—"

"That it is very cold."

"Yes. In fact, it is freezing." The stranger shivered slightly and drew his cloak closer around his shoulders. "Do you play?" he asked.

"A little," said Pierre, who felt somehow reassured by the mere fact that the other had spoken to him.

The waiter brought cards and another bottle of wine, and Pierre moved over to the other's table.

For a half-hour the game proceeded, for the most part in silence. Once or twice Pierre glanced at his watch, then up at the window, which from his viewpoint disclosed only a glimpse of dark, gloomy sky and the upper framework of the Pont de Suresnes. Gradually, as the waiter continued to replace empty bottles with full ones, the stranger's tongue was loosened.

"You're lucky," said he, eyeing the little heap of silver and small notes at Pierre's elbow.

Pierre glanced again at his watch. "Let us hope so," he muttered.

"And yet you are uneasy and agitated. That is wrong. Learn, my friend, the value of philosophy—of stoicism." The stranger waved a hand in the air and grinned foolishly. "Learn to control your fate. For whatever happens today, or tomorrow, you are still a man."

Pierre's uneasiness returned. "You are drunk," he said calmly. "But what do you mean?"

The other pointed a wavering finger at Pierre's hand. "That's what I mean. You tremble, you glance about, you are afraid. No doubt you have a reason; but look at that!" He held out his own hand, which shook like a leaf in the wind. "Observe my steadiness, my calm! And yet my whole future—my whole future is decided within the hour."

"Come," said Pierre, "you talk too much, my friend."

"You are mistaken," said the other with some dignity. "I do not talk too much. I never have talked too much." He laid his cards on the table, picked up his glass and drained it. "Monsieur, I like you. I think I shall tell you a great secret."

"I advise you to keep it to yourself," said Pierre, who was beginning to be bored. He glanced again at his watch. It was a quarter to six.

"Right. Unquestionably right," said the stranger. "The greatest of all virtues is caution." He extended his arm as though to pluck a measure of that quality from the thick, damp air. "At the present moment I am a glowing example of the value of caution. It is the *sine qua non* of success. My motto is 'In words bold, in action prudent.' Caution! Prudence! I thank you, my friend."

This, being somewhat at variance with Pierre's theory of life, slightly aroused him. "But one cannot be an absolute coward," he protested.

"*Eh, bien,*" returned the other, raising his brows in

scorn at the bare suggestion, "one is expected to be a man. But what would you have? There are times—there is always one's safety. Preservation is the first law of existence. Now I, for instance"—he leaned forward and finished in a confidential whisper—"would never think of blaming a man for obtaining a substitute to fight a duel for him. A mere matter of caution. Would you?"

Pierre felt a choking lump rise to his throat, and when he tried to speak found himself unable to open his mouth. All was known! He was lost! This drunken fellow—who probably was not drunk at all—who was he? Undoubtedly, Phillips had betrayed him. And then, as he sat stunned by surprise, the other continued:

"The truth is—you see, my friend, I trust you, and I want your opinion—that is exactly what I have done myself. It was to be at six o'clock," he said. "And he—that fool of a Dumain—proposed for us to mask. That was what gave me the idea."

A thought darted into Pierre's brain like a leaping flame, and forced from him an unguarded exclamation: "Aha! Lamon!"

The other glanced up with quick suspicion. "How do you know that?" he demanded thickly.

But Pierre had had a second in which to recover his wits. "A man as famous as you?" he asked in a tone of surprise. "Everyone knows Lamon."

The uneasiness on the other's face gave way to a fatuous smile. "Perhaps," he admitted.

Pierre's brain, always nimble in an emergency, was working rapidly. He glanced at his watch: there still remained ten minutes before Phillips could be expected to arrive. As for this drunken Lamon, there was nothing to be feared from him. Then a new fear assailed him.

"But what if your substitute is wounded?"

Lamon's lips, tightly compressed in an effort at control, relaxed in a knowing grin. "Impossible." He fumbled in his vest pockets and finally drew forth a card, which he tossed on the table in front of Pierre. "You see, he's an expert."

Pierre, turning the card over, read it in a single glance:

ALBERT PHILLIPS
Professeur d'Escrime
Méthode Américaine

A TYRANT ABDICATES

The fact that Mrs. Coit kept her rooms full could be accounted for only by the Law of Chance. As a matter of free choice, no rational human being would ever have submitted to her sour tutelage. But situated as it was, on East Thirty-seventh Street, her house had inevitably attracted a certain portion of those poor unfortunates who find in that locality everything of home that New York can mean to them; and what Mrs. Coit got she usually kept. Her manner was so very forbidding that it seemed even to forbid their escape.

Perhaps the most unpopular of Mrs. Coit's activities was the strict supervision of the movements of her men roomers. It came to be generally understood that coming in at eleven o'clock was barely safe, midnight required a thorough explanation, and one o'clock was unpardonable. From this you may judge of the rest.

The two who suffered most from this stern maternalism were the Boy and the Girl. It is unnecessary to give their names, since, being in love, they were undistinguishable from several million other boys and girls that the world has seen or read about. To confirm their title as members of this club, their course of true love did not run smooth. No doubt it is trying enough to be bothered by a particular mother, a strict father, or an inquisitive aunt; but all of these are as nothing to a prying landlady.

Mrs. Coit was fat, forty, and unfair. No one knew the nature of her widowhood, whether simple or complex, voluntary or forced, but all were agreed that Mr. Coit was lucky to escape, through whatever medium. The Book-keeper had once declared positively that Mrs. Coit was a *grass* widow, but, being pressed for an explanation, admitted that he had grounded his belief on no better foundation than the too evident presence of dry hay in the mattresses.

The roomers—that is, the seasoned ones—were little disturbed by her. Most of them had come to accept life as a dull and colorless routine, to which the impression of anything unusual came as a relief; and Mrs. Coit served as matter for continual amusement. They laughed at her and submitted to her minute censorship without complaint.

But in each of these dulled and sluggish hearts old Romance crouched, ever watchful for an opportunity to make its presence known. That opportunity arrived on the day that the Boy first met the Girl.

Within a week every roomer in the house was enlisted on the side of Cupid. It is true that Cupid needed no assistance, especially from these dried-up mortals whom he had long ago abandoned; but they *thought* they helped, and Cupid always was an ungrateful little wretch. The Boy was fair, the Girl was sweet, and it truly seemed that it would take much more than the grim visage of Mrs. Coit to frighten away that ever-welcome though sometimes painful visitor.

Mrs. Coit, however, was doing her best. After ten years of unchallenged tyranny, her subjects openly rebelled and resented her malicious activity. As I have said, for themselves they did not care—what mattered a little extra discomfort in lives long since devoted to the Prosaic? But when it came to the Boy and the Girl, and interference with the divine right of rings, they rallied round the flag and struck hard for the colors of Love.

As time passed and the general interest in the affair deepened, Mrs. Coit redoubled her vigilance and asperity. Her remarks to the Boy on the foolishness of marrying at his age and on his salary were repeated with emphasis, and to the Girl she talked so severely about the selfishness of hampering the Boy's career that she left her in tears. This was unwise; it merely served as an excuse to the Boy for so many more kisses.

Many were the objections entered by Mrs. Coit, many were the petty trials and inconveniences she managed to inflict on the lovers; all, of course, in vain. The women declared that she was jealous of the Boy, which was manifestly absurd; the men, that she was naturally mean, which was somewhat ungallant. Anyway, they might have spared their abuses, since the Boy and the Girl had finally been steered through the shoals of criticism and the rocks of opposition to the sheltered harbor of a Definite Engagement. Mrs. Coit had settled down to a dull resentment; the roomers, to a calm and pleasurable expectation.

Mrs. Coit, on her daily round of dusting, was commenting to herself somewhat bitterly on the folly of youth and the general levity of mankind. In the Bookkeeper's room she grew particularly resentful, since he had only the day before advised her to mind her own business, and jabbing the duster savagely at a corner of the mantel, she knocked to the floor a little plaster bust of Milton, which broke into a dozen pieces. Sobered by this unhousewifely incident, she proceeded to the Boy's room, next door.

She entered without knocking, and to her surprise found

the Boy sitting on the edge of the bed with his face buried in his hands. Mrs. Coit regarded him silently, with increasing wrath. The Boy, not hearing her enter, remained motionless.

"Well!" said Mrs. Coit finally, "Ain't you goin' to work?"

The Boy looked up. "No."

His eyes were swollen with sleeplessness and his face was pale, his hair uncombed, his whole figure dejected and forlorn.

Mrs. Coit noted each of these symptoms separately and carefully.

"Lose your job?" she asked, almost hopefully.

The Boy shook his head, and buried it again in his hands. Mrs. Coit, trying to maintain her attitude of severe disapproval, began to dust the Morris chair. Then, after discovering that she had gone over the same arm four times, she turned to the Boy again,

"Sick?" she demanded.

"No," said the Boy, without moving. Evidently he was not looking for sympathy.

Mrs. Coit regarded him critically. No, he certainly wasn't drunk. Not *him*. Then, glancing over the bed, her eye fell on a photograph in a little gilt frame. It showed the face of the Boy, smiling, happy.

Mrs. Coit understood at once. For five long months this same photograph had been staring at her from the dressing table in the Girl's room, on the floor below. To confirm her suspicion, she looked at the mantel, where a picture of the Girl had occupied the place of honor. It was not there.

Mrs. Coit gazed at the picture for a full minute, then without a word completed her dusting and prepared to leave the room. The Boy remained silent. Mrs. Coit, her hand on the doorknob, turned and looked at him hesitatingly. Then,

"Have you had a fight with *her*?" she demanded.

The Boy looked up at her despairingly. "What do you care?" he cried. His voice was harsh and shrill with pain.

Mrs. Coit started to answer, then, thinking better of it, turned and fled down the hall, banging the door after her. The Boy snatched up the picture, pulled off its frame, tore it in a dozen pieces, and threw them on the floor.

Fifteen minutes later Mrs. Coit, passing through the lower hall, heard the outer door open, and, looking down the stairway, saw the Boy go out and close the door after him. Then, muttering to herself something about "idiot," and holding the duster firmly before her after the manner of a fixed bayonet, she proceeded to the Girl's room and entered with an air of determination.

Here the havoc was even greater. The Girl, reclining limply and disconsolately in an easy chair, eyes inflamed, cheeks marked with tear-tracks and splotches of red, turned and looked at the intruder indifferently.

"I knew it," said Mrs. Coit, in a tone of deep satisfaction. "Why ain't you at work?"

The Girl tried to smile. "I have a headache," she said.

Mrs. Coit snorted contemptuously. "Oh, I know all about it," she declared. "He just told me. I knew it'd be like this."

The Girl covered her face with her hands and turned away.

"I knew it'd be like this," repeated Mrs. Coit.

The Girl made no sign.

"What'd you want to fight about a little thing like that for?" Mrs. Coit asked cunningly.

"It didn't seem little then," said the Girl wearily.

Mrs. Coit pressed her advantage, but to no purpose. The Girl refused to give any information; she even refused to become angry. Finally, at the insistence of Mrs. Coit, she dressed herself and prepared to go to the office.

"You'd better walk around a while before you go in," said Mrs. Coit. "Your face looks like a boiled cucumber."

After she had gone Mrs. Coit sat in the chair she had left, gazing thoughtfully at some little bits of paper scattered on the floor. What she was thinking, no one could possibly have told. Her face expressed nothing but grimness, her attitude satisfaction; and as she stooped over to gather up the bits of paper her lips settled into what might have been a line of triumphant resolve.

That evening, for the first time in many months, the Boy returned from the office alone. He and the Girl had walked together always—but that was over. However much he loved her, he still felt that she had said to him that which could never be forgiven, especially since it was undeserved. Of course, if she came to him and *asked* forgiveness—he caught his breath at the thought—but that, he was sure, she would never do.

His day at the office had been miserable, and the future, he reflected, held nothing for him but a dreary succession of similar ones. He had decided to leave Mrs. Coit's that very evening, since everything there would be full of bittersweet memories of the one happy period of his life. One has great capacity for grief, as for joy, at twenty-one.

As he was turning the key in the lock of the outer door, a figure came up the steps. It was the Girl.

Without speaking, the Boy opened the door and stood aside politely to allow her to pass. She bowed her head in thanks, and silently began to ascend the stairs to her room.

The Boy's voice came after her, calling her name. She turned and looked down at him. He was standing by the mail rack, holding a large envelope in his hand.

"Is it for me?" asked the Girl doubtfully.

"No," said the Boy. "It's for—us."

Her face flushed at the familiar pronoun.

The Boy ascended the stairs to where she stood.

"I suppose we must open it together," he continued coldly. "It's addressed to both of us."

The Girl looked on silently while he tore open the envelope. His elbow brushed her arm, and they both started nervously.

Then, as they gazed together at the card the envelope had contained, they blushed almost painfully. The Boy felt his heart mount to his throat; the Girl put up her hand to brush away the mist that suddenly formed before her eyes. Pasted side by side on the card were the two photographs they had that morning torn up and thrown away, and written below in a shaky, curious hand was the inscription:

> To two young fools
> from an old fool.

And tied to the card with a piece of faded blue ribbon was an old, well-worn wedding ring!

Fifteen minutes later the Boy and the Girl came down, hand in hand, to the sitting room where Mrs. Coit sat poring over her account books. She rose at their approach.

"Well?" she demanded aggressively.

The Boy, nothing daunted, advanced boldly, holding one hand toward her.

"Here is your ring, Mrs. Coit," he said, the old happy smile in his eyes. "I thought you might want it back again."

Mrs. Coit hesitated, and for the first time in the knowledge of Thirty-seventh Street seemed embarrassed.

"That ain't my ring," said she finally.

Then occurred the outrage. Perhaps she wouldn't have minded so much, but just at that moment the Bookkeeper passed through the hall, and, glancing in at the door, saw everything. The Boy threw his arms around Mrs. Coit's neck, gave her a resounding kiss on either cheek, and, leaving the ring lying on the desk, fled toward the stairs, the Girl following.

Mrs. Coit recovered in time to pursue them to the foot of the stairs.

"Hey, there!" she called, a curious break in the voice she tried to make stern. "Hey, there! You left your room in a pretty fix this morning, you did! Once more like that, and out you go!"

From the floor above came the sound of happy, mocking laughter. Mrs. Coit's reign had ended.

An Agacella Or

George Stafford had been—believe him—from his infancy a most unique and interesting personality. But if you will believe me instead, he had been nothing of the sort.

I know very well the conclusion at which you will immediately arrive when I say that George Stafford was phlegmatic. But you will be wrong. In these days of extreme specialization, even our adjectives are not free; it has come to the place where nothing can properly be called occult except a science, nothing can be high—in the figurative sense—except ideals, and no one can be phlegmatic except a Dutchman. Nevertheless, in spite of the facts that he was born in Plainfield, New Jersey, that he spoke nothing but United States (being as ignorant of English as he was of Sanskrit), and that his father had made some half a million dollars solely through the benevolent protection of the New York Custom House, George Stafford was phlegmatic. More than that, he was unimaginative, he considered billiards a rather violent form of exercise, and, if the truth be told, he was even a trifle stupid.

To let you at once into the secrets of George's mind and character, it is only necessary to say that he was spending his vacation at the Hotel Thiersberry, in the Berkshires. With the single exception of an orchestra chair in a New York theater, the Hotel Thiersberry is admitted to be the very dullest spot in all America. It is eminently proper, fearfully expensive, and in the last degree exclusive. "Exclusive" is a terrible word, and the Hotel Thiersberry is a terrible place. And it was here that George Stafford was spending his vacation.

I use the term "vacation" merely for the sake of politeness. For, consulting my dictionary, I find that a vacation is an intermission of stated employment, and it would be absurd to imagine George as consorting with anything so vulgar as stated employment. Not that he was spiritualistic or esthetic or artistic; work—or anything else—could never have disturbed George's soul; but it would most certainly have disturbed his body. And yet he had an excuse—such as it was—for his use of the word "vacation." For, having existed through thirty years in a state of habitual and supreme idleness, George had been persuaded by a friend to put on at least the semblance of endeavor, and had submitted to the painting of a sign, "Rainier & Stafford, Architects," on the door of a modest suite on the fifty-eighth floor of a downtown skyscraper. The check which the elder Stafford drew each month to help pay George's share of the office expenses was surprisingly small, everything considered.

It was through the influence of Rainier, his partner, that George had been permitted to enter the jealous portals of the Hotel Thiersberry; for the House of Stafford, though favorably known on Mercer Street, was beyond the pale socially. It had not yet arrived. George, though idle, had never been fashionably idle; indeed, that is an art that is seldom acquired as early as the second generation. Thus it was that upon registering at the Hotel Thiersberry George had found himself entering on an entirely new phase of existence.

It was not at all the same as an ordinary hotel. To mention only one peculiarity, George found soon after his arrival, on going into the library to write a letter to his partner, that there was no letter paper. On investigation, he learned that at the Hotel Thiersberry one was supposed to be desirous of using one's own letter paper. George had none, and he distinctly desired to write a letter; in fact, now that he came to think of it, several of them.

The third morning of his vacation found George in the library, writing letters. He had bought the paper the day before, in a shop in the village, five miles away. He was half-ashamed to use it, and it was indeed very unusual paper; but the shop had contained nothing else that was even possible. This that he had finally chosen was tinted a magnificent purple, and there was embossed in flaming gold at the top of each sheet the figure of an animal that greatly resembled a cow, holding in its hoofs what appeared to be a bundle of kindling wood. It was one of those atrocities which you may see in any stationery shop window; and even George, deficient in taste as he was, had been almost tempted to buy a linen tablet instead.

George was writing on the large mahogany table in the center of the library. Seated opposite him was the lank and angular Mrs. Gerard-Lee, copying a list of synonyms from Graves; for Mrs. Gerard-Lee was an authority. Over by a window were young Mr. Amblethwaite and Miss Lorry Carson, engaged in a hot dispute concerning the proper shape of legs, it being understood that the legs were supposed to be attached to a Pelton saddler; while in front of the door leading to the veranda were gathered a half-dozen old females representing at least twelve hundred pounds avoirdupois and about twelve million sterling. "How Mother would enjoy this!" thought George. And he wrote:

*   *   *

I just overheard Mrs. Scott-Wickersham say that she returned to America a month later than usual in order to attend the Duchess of Wimbledon's masque ball. And yet she doesn't seem—

At this moment George became aware of the fact that someone was standing at his right elbow. Turning, he beheld a middle-aged lady of impressive build and a somewhat florid countenance peering through a lorgnette at the sheets of letter paper lying before him. At his movement, her gaze slowly traveled from the paper to his upturned face.

"Sir," she said, "what is your name?"

"What?" said George, taken aback. "My—oh, yes, my name—of course, certainly, my name." Then, somewhat recovering himself, "Stafford is my name," he said with dignity.

His questioner regarded him with a look of triumph. "It is he," she said to herself, aloud. "I am sure of it, since he can't remember his name." Whereupon she winked at George distinctly, even painfully.

Now, George had learned in the last three days that one must be willing to undergo a certain amount of humiliation when one is breaking into the Hotel Thiersberry. But to have a strange lady stand before you and make remarks about you to your face and wink at you was too much. He opened his mouth to protest, but before he could speak, the lady continued. "Mr. Stafford," she said, "I am Mrs. Gordon Wheeler, of Lenox; and this is my daughter. . . . Cecily, Mr. Stafford."

Whatever protest George had decided to utter was drowned in amazement as Mrs. Gordon Wheeler stepped aside to make way for her daughter. For the first time in quite ten years he became conscious of the blood in his veins. While he stood half-dazed by the vision of loveliness disclosed by Mrs. Wheeler's timely eclipse, Cecily, her cheeks a delightful rosy pink, stepped up to him with outstretched hands.

"Mr. Stafford," she said in a low, sweet voice. And then she stopped, as if finding it impossible to express her feelings in words.

"My dear girl," said George, taking the hands and holding on to them, "if you will sit in this chair for a few minutes, till I finish my letter, I shall be ready to talk to you. I trust your mother sleeps in the afternoon?"

"Good heavens!" said Mrs. Wheeler. "Here I am with an unmarried daughter, and the man accuses me of sleeping! My dear sir, it is impossible. In these days of the vulgar competition of the *nouveau riche*, one must be constantly on one's guard. However, I often close my eyes."

"I am sure you do," said George approvingly; and then, under his breath, "Goodness knows they need it!"

"You will eat at our table?" asked Mrs. Wheeler.

"Certainly," said George, "and thank you."

After Mrs. Wheeler had gone, it took George a full hour to finish the letter to his mother. Within two minutes, Cecily, seated beside him, became impatient and began lassoing the toe of her slipper with the cord of her handbag; and George, wanting an excuse to gaze at the slipper, which was worth it, offered a wager that she couldn't do it once in ten.

"That is very silly," said Cecily, "as I have been walking and am covered with dust."

"My dear girl—" began George, embarrassed.

"You called me that before," Cecily interrupted, "and I don't like it. And now, if you don't mind, I shall read while you finish your letter." But she raised her eyes every few seconds to see if George was through writing, which accounts for the fact that he spoiled four sheets of the wonderfully embossed paper with blots, and found himself writing upside down on the fifth.

The early afternoon found George and Cecily together in a canoe on the lake in front of the hotel. The water was still and crystal clear, save where here and there a leaping trout or bass disturbed its surface. Above their heads the overhanging boughs swayed gently back and forth with the sinuous grace of an Indian punkah; and the water trickled from the up-sprung leaves with a soothing, continuous music. George, leaning back contentedly, lit a cigarette—his fifth in half an hour—and blew caressing rings around the neck of a greedy swan.

"Aren't you afraid you'll get overheated?" said Cecily sarcastically.

"No," said George, in innocent surprise. "It's perfectly safe here in the shade. Really, I'm quite cool."

Cecily sat up straight and regarded him with speechless indignation. "Do you think," she finally demanded, "that I came out in this boat to sit and watch you smoke? Look at that!"—pointing across the lake, where another canoe could be seen shooting along the father shore. "They started after we did. You ought to be ashamed of yourself. Take me back to the hotel."

At this command George sat up and regarded his companion with surprise. "What the dickens have I done?" he demanded. "What's the trouble?"

"The trouble is," said Cecily severely, "that this is a canoe and not a houseboat. It's supposed to move. This swaying motion which I experience whenever you shift to a more comfortable position is no doubt very delightful, but I can get the same effect in a rocking chair, where there is no danger of being spilled into the water at every—"

"Do you mean," George interrupted, "that you want to cross the lake?"

"I do," said Cecily decidedly.

The young man sat up again, this time quite erect, and surveyed his companion with unfeigned astonishment. "Good heavens!" he said. "What for? Look at that!"—pointing to the float at the bottom of the steps leading to the hotel. It was quite two hundred feet away. "Haven't we come all the way from there to here? I know we drifted, but we came, didn't we? Anyway, why should we want to get anywhere? I don't see why you want to go so fast."

Cecily regarded him with unmixed contempt. "Very well," she said finally. "If you will hand me that paddle, I shall return to the hotel. I suppose I must take you too, since you're too heavy to throw overboard. Give me the paddle, please."

At last George was aroused. Now, there was not less than two hundred pounds of George; and a mass of two hundred pounds, when once aroused, can do almost anything with a canoe. Within ten seconds of the commencement of the young man's unwonted and sudden activity, the canoe was resting on the surface of the lake bottom upwards, with Cecily clinging desperately on one end, and George on the other.

"I *asked* you to hand me the paddle," said Cecily in chilling tones.

George glared at her across the shiny bottom. "Here it is," said he grimly, reaching for it as it floated by some two feet away.

"Be careful!" screamed Cecily; whereupon George, losing his hold on the canoe, floundered frantically about like a young whale, causing Cecily's end, with Cecily attached, to sink some four or five feet into the lake. When she emerged, dripping with water and pink with rage, George had again caught hold of the canoe, and was trying to hold on to the paddle and wipe the water from his eyes with one hand.

"I suppose," said Cecily, with withering contempt, "that you can swim?"

"I can," said George, "but I hate to."

"I honestly believe that, if I could, you would let me tow you ashore."

"No-o"—doubtfully. "But if you could go to the hotel and get someone to fetch a boat——"

Cecily was speechless. Without another word, she gave the canoe a push against George's breast, and started swimming toward the float with one hand, guiding her cargo with the other. George floated calmly on his back, eyeing the performance with admiring approval. By virtue of his position, he arrived at the float first; and, clambering upon it, he pulled first Cecily, and then the canoe, out after him.

"That was a jolly ducking, wasn't it?" he said pleasantly.

During the week that followed, George Stafford was subjected, for the first time in his life, to discipline. Far from being offended at his willingness to be towed ashore, Cecily seemed to take an even deeper interest in him, and lost no time in undertaking his reformation. After many attempts, she found his wits incapable of exercise; but she had less difficulty with his arms and legs. By the end of the week he presented almost an athletic appearance, though it is true that he was eternally out of breath.

Behold him, then, on a Friday afternoon, dressed in flannels and batting wildly at a tennis ball which Cecily always managed to send just beyond his reach. George's flannels were not immaculate—he tumbled too often in his vain lunges after the ball—his face was dripping with perspiration, and his collar had somewhat the appearance of a lettuce salad. Cecily stopped suddenly with her racket uplifted ready to serve, and began to laugh.

"What's the matter?" her opponent demanded.

"Nothing," said Cecily, "only——" and then she laughed again.

"Look a' here," said George hotly, "if you think——"

"But I don't. I can't. Are you tired?"

"No!"—indignantly.

"Well, I am. Besides, I want to talk. I've just thought of something I want to tell you."

"What is it?" asked George, after they had walked over

to a tree and seated themselves in the shade. He was lying
flat on his back, with a cigarette between his lips, blinking
stupidly at a fleecy, puffed-up cloud that showed through
a rift in the leaves. Cecily, seated beside him, was idly
stuffing the pocket of his shirt with grass. When she spoke
it was in a slow, impressive tone.

"Mamma suspects," said she.

George turned and looked at her uneasily. "Suspects
what?"

"Why," said Cecily, embarrassed, "don't you know?
Our—my—us."

"Oh!" said George, in a tone of relief. Then, raising
himself to his elbow in irritation, "I don't like people who
suspect," he declared. "It's uncomfortable, and it's dangerous, and it's bad form. Now, I never suspect anyone.
Why should she?"

"Perhaps she saw us."

"When?"

"Last night. You remember you kissed me good-
night on the veranda, and then followed me up to the hall
and——"

"All right," said George; "that settles it. I'm through.
If every time you turn around——"

"Don't be silly," Cecily interrupted impatiently. "You
know we've got to tell her."

"My dear girl," said George, "*we* have nothing to do
with it. It's *you*. You pulled me ashore. You made me
play tennis. You called me George. And now—it's up to
you."

"But I've tried, and I can't. I really can't."

"Very well," said George. "Then, we'll have to call it
off. Rather than face that—your mother, I'll go away from
here and never see you again. You're killing me, anyway.
Look at that sun! I've been out in it for three hours, when
I should have been asleep. I've done nothing but work
ever since I met you. I wake up in the morning all ready
for a good rest, and here you are at the door loaded down

with paddles and rods and lines. You can't even let the fish alone. And if you think for a minute that I——"

"All right," said Cecily. "I'll tell her. But you'll have to be with me."

Accordingly, nine o'clock of that evening found a young man and a girl walking hand in hand down the corridor in the Hotel Thiersberry which led to the apartments of Mrs. Gordon Wheeler. They walked slowly, even timidly. As they passed an elevator shaft, the young man might have been observed glancing at it longingly; whereupon the girl tightened her grasp on his hand and hurried her step.

The loud bang of a door stopped them halfway down the hall. Then came heavy footsteps; and they stood still, hesitating, while the ponderous form of Mrs. Gordon Wheeler bore down upon them from the direction of her rooms.

"There you are!" exclaimed Mrs. Wheeler, in the tone of one who has made an important, if not wholly pleasing, discovery.

"We are, indeed," agreed George, with admirable presence of mind.

Mrs. Wheeler paused, regarding the pair sternly with set lips, then pointed silently to the door of her rooms.

"We can't talk here," she said.

"Now," she continued, after they were seated inside the apartment, "what have you to say for yourself?"

"Mrs. Wheeler," said George, "in view of the eloquence of your eyes, I am silent. I am sure there is something you wish to say to me."

"Young man, are you entirely without morals?"

"I hope so. They are inconvenient. Have I ever given you reason to doubt it?" demanded George.

"Don't be funny," Mrs. Wheeler said sternly. "This is no laughing matter. Don't try to be witty, sir."

"He won't, Mamma," put in Cecily. "I can promise you that."

"Be silent, child! You don't know what you've escaped," said her mother. "As for you"—turning to George—"what do you think of this?"

George took the slip—a newspaper clipping—and read it through. "Well, what of it?" he demanded.

"Of course you don't understand it," said Mrs. Wheeler sarcastically. "I am surprised—I am really surprised—at your shamelessness. Listen." She read aloud from the newspaper clipping:

"The Earl of Woodstock, who has been staying since early July at the Severance villa in Newport, is reported to have retreated to a hotel in the Berkshires for a month's rest. He is preserving a strict incognito, having been advised by his physicians to obtain absolute quiet, if possible."

"Well," said George, "it's a good thing for the Earl that Cecily didn't get hold of him."

Mrs. Wheeler, ignoring him, walked to her writing desk and took from the top thereof a large book bound in red leather.

"That," she said, pointing to the clipping she had just read, "was in the *Herald* two weeks ago. It naturally led me to investigate, since Cecily and I also had arranged to come to the Berkshires, and among other information I found the following"—reading aloud from the book:

"Woodstock, Earl of, and Baron Dynely of Aldingbourne, county Oxford, in England; an agecella or, pied sable, armed, unguled, and bearing rods. *Virtus dedit, cura servabit.*"

"Now," said Mrs. Wheeler, closing the book and dropping it on the table with a bang that caused Cecily to jump clear out of her chair, "what do you think of that?"

"Fine," said George approvingly. "Quite interesting. What does it mean?"

"It means that you're an impostor," said Mrs. Wheeler, glaring at him. "But, thank God, I've found you out in time! One week after that notice appeared in the *Herald* I walked into the library of this hotel. What did I see? I saw a fat, overfed, and foolish-looking young man writing letters. Looking closer, I saw that the paper he was using bore a crest consisting of an agacella or, armed, and bearing rods."

"It was nothing of the sort," said George hotly. "It was a cow getting ready to light a fire."

"Don't interrupt," said Mrs. Wheeler. "Don't you think I know an agacella when I see one? I asked the young man his name. It took him quite two minutes to think of it. On questioning him further, I discovered that he was completely an ass. The conclusion was inevitable: it was the Earl of Woodstock!"

"It was nothing of the sort!" said George again, indignantly. "It was me!"

"Of course," Mrs. Wheeler went on, again ignoring him, "I immediately introduced him to my daughter. Cecily—dear child—did her part nobly. She became your constant companion. You became inseparable. And just as I was preparing to send to London to find out what repairs were needed at your town house, I look over my evening's mail, and I find—this!" She snatched up a newspaper from a heap on the desk and read aloud from its columns:

"The Earl of Woodstock, who has been taking a much-needed rest at the Hope cottage in the Berkshires, has returned to the Severance villa at Newport."

"Now," said Mrs. Wheeler, pointing an accusing finger at George, "who are you?"

"That was the first question you asked me," said George. "Are you going to begin all over again? Because if you are——" He rose and picked up his hat.

"No, you don't," said Mrs. Wheeler grimly, getting between him and the door. "You wait till I'm through with you."

"George!" cried Cecily. "Are you going to leave me?"

George, incapable of the exertion required to stand and talk at the same time, reseated himself.

"Cecily," said he, "you ask too much of me. I could forgive you anything but your choice of a mother. That was your great mistake. As it is, we must part. I shall never see you again. The fact that we are married makes no difference."

"Married!" shrieked Mrs. Wheeler, dropping upon a divan and clutching wildly at the air.

"Yes, married," said George calmly. "Married by a fool of a parson in the village yonder. Cecily has won me. She had rather a hard time of it, and so did I. I'm completely tired out. The truth is, I was in a state of utter exhaustion, and didn't realize what I was doing. I was in no condition to resist."

Mrs. Wheeler arose, trembling, resting her hand on her bosom tragically. "Mr. Stafford," she said, "this is incredible. I can scarcely believe my ears. As for you, Cecily, you shall hear from me; but not now—not tonight. I am inexpressibly shocked. My nerves are completely upset. Tomorrow we shall talk the matter over and do the best we can with this awful mess. Good night." She walked falteringly to the door of her bedroom and disappeared within.

"George," said Cecily, walking over to him and taking his hands in her own, "do you love me?"

"Of course I do," said George. "Haven't I proved it?"

Cecily stopped and kissed his cheek. "I don't mind it a bit because you're not an earl, dear," she said tenderly. "You're stupid enough to be one."

A LITTLE
LOVE AFFAIR

❧

Mr. Bob Chidden sat on a box in the September sun-shine, in the back court of a private dwelling in West Twenty-third Street, long since converted into a rooming house. He had for some time been examining the worn toes of his boots with a stare of melancholy interest. On his head was a broad-brimmed straw hat of a dingy color, with a crack in the crown; to his form and limbs there hung a faded blue shirt and a pair of shiny black trousers; he held in his hand the handle of a dilapidated broom. Suddenly, as a soft sound came from behind, he removed his gaze from the boots and twisted his neck, and beheld a large gray cat advancing cautiously and dain-tily along the cement walk.

"Fuzzy thing!" said Mr. Chidden, in a tone of deep contempt. Then he turned around with a hasty glance at the kitchen window. No one was in sight.

"Disgustin' animal!" said Mr. Chidden, and gave a vi-cious poke with the broom handle. The cat leaped aside with a snarl, and disappeared up the side of the fence. Mr.

Chidden allowed himself a momentary grin of appreciation, then sighed and resumed the melancholy stare at the toes of his boots. Five minutes passed.

"Robert!" came a sudden voice, harsh and authoritative, from the kitchen door.

Mr. Chidden rose to his feet and faced about. In the doorway appeared the form of a woman, angular, red-faced, something above fifty. She had the appearance of that class of females who manage somehow to exist in a perpetual state of agitation; and at this moment her emotion was apparent in every feature of her forbidding countenance.

"Well?" said Mr. Chidden.

The lady snorted. "Didn't you hear the bell ring?"

"I did not."

"Well, it did. Answer it. I'm too busy."

Mr. Chidden proceeded through the kitchen and lower hall, up a flight of stairs, and down another hall to the front door. There he found a boy from the tailor shop at the corner, who announced, in a squeaky voice, that he had come for Mr. Stubbs' suit. Mr. Chidden mounted two flights of stairs to the third-floor front and returned with a heap of gray material hanging over his arm.

"Be ready in half an hour," said the boy, taking the suit. "Tell Mr. Stubbs he'll have to send for it. I got to go to school."

Mr. Chidden nodded and closed the door. As he did so, a voice floated up from the kitchen:

"Robert!"

Mr. Chidden halted abruptly, while the settled melancholy of his face deepened to an expression of despair.

"It's too much!" he muttered aloud. "I'll revolt, that's what I'll do, I'll revolt!" Then he sighed, thrust his hands deep in his trousers pockets, and descended to the kitchen.

"Have you removed that coal?" demanded the red-faced woman, as he entered.

"What coal?" inquired Mr. Chidden.

"Lord save us!" grunted the lady. "*The* coal! Are you without brains, Robert Chidden? If ever woman were hangin' on the neck of a worthless brother, you're it. Go and move that coal!"

"You ain't hangin' on my neck," protested Mr. Chidden, with some energy. "You ain't hangin' on my neck, Maria Chidden."

"I'm not, perhaps, in a way," agreed Miss Chidden. "As a figure of speech, which you don't understand, I am, and have been for twenty years. But I've got no time for argument. Go and move that coal!"

For a single moment Mr. Chidden's brain entertained a giddy and audacious thought. The words, "I won't move coal," were formed in his throat. But, alas! they stuck there. He turned without a word, took the key to the cellar door from a nail on the wall, and made his way to the regions below. There, at the end toward the street, he found a large pile of coal which had been dumped in through the sidewalk, and which it was his painful duty to move with a shovel and basket to the vicinity of the furnace, some forty feet away. Mr. Chidden set about the unpleasant task with a dogged and gloomy air. It was easy to see that his heart was not in the work.

Little wonder, for even his sister Maria would have admitted, if absolutely pushed, that Mr. Chidden was not born to move coal. Indeed, at one time in their lives—when, on the death of their father, they had found themselves in undisputed possession of an inheritance of six thousand dollars—she had regarded him as an equal. But when he had taken his half and gone up to New Rochelle to open a haberdasher shop, she had allowed herself certain dark observations concerning the state of his intellect; and when the haberdasher shop had failed and left its enterprising founder penniless, the observations had become painful convictions, declared with painful directness.

Twenty long years had passed since Mr. Chidden, finding his inheritance gone and with it all his youthful ardor, had come to live with his sister in the rooming house she had established with a portion of her share of the patrimony. At first he had intended to make it merely a temporary visit, to recuperate his powers; but time had drifted on. At the end of a year he had become a fixed institution, and had remained so ever since. Several times he had made a desperate and spasmodic attempt to break away by getting a job of one sort or another, but the difficulties and disappointments encountered in each instance had filled him with the settled conviction that fate had marked him for the victim of a cruel and remorseless tyranny. He gave up altogether, and became a furnace tender and handyman around the house.

Now and then, during the twenty years of horror, Mr. Chidden had lashed his sinking spirit to the point of rebellion. Once he had openly and fearlessly run away, only to be driven back by stern necessity in less than a fortnight. On another occasion he had conceived a bold and brilliant plan; and, after cogitating on it for two weeks and—more specifically—having fortified himself with a glass of blackberry cordial surreptitiously procured from a bottle in the sideboard, he had advanced a certain proposition to his sister Maria.

"My money!" Miss Chidden had exclaimed, after gazing at her brother for two minutes in dazed stupefaction at his unspeakable temerity. "Give you *my* money to throw away, Robert Chidden! I'm not crazy, thank you."

"But it's a chance," Mr. Chidden had argued desperately. "I tell you it's a real chance, Maria. Fine little shop—Seventh Avenue—has to sell—forty percent—can't lose. It wouldn't cost more than a thousand—fifteen hundred at the outside. You wouldn't miss it. You must have ten thousand by this time. Where is it? Railroads, I suppose. Six percent. Is it railroads?"

"No, it ain't. And if you think——"

"It don't matter," said Mr. Chidden, actually interrupting her in the excitement of his feelings. "I'm your own brother, Maria. I'd pay you back in a year. Eight percent. Wouldn't you take eight percent from your own brother? You wouldn't miss it out of ten thousand."

"You're right," said Miss Chidden grimly. "I won't miss it, Robert. I won't miss it *at* all. It may be ten thousand, and it may be more, and it may be less, but whatever it is, I'll keep it. It ain't in railroads, and it pays some better than six per cent. When I invest money, I don't put it where them Wall Street robbers can peck at it. Neither do I give it to a lummox like you to throw away. Now you go out and clean off the sidewalk."

"But, Maria——" Mr. Chidden began, almost tearfully.

"Robert! There's the broom."

That had been the last eruption of the spirit of revolt in Mr. Chidden's bosom. The fire still smoldered, but it gave off nothing but smoke—mutterings and moody thoughts. The chief pity of this proceeded from the fact that he was constitutionally a cheerful man. For two weeks following the unpleasant episode related above, he had endeavored to drown his discontent by frequent sippings of the blackberry cordial; then his sister, actuated by a mean suspicion, had put a lock on the sideboard door, and he had been denied even that medicinal solace.

The amazing part of it was that Mr. Chidden was able to preserve the faintest trace of individuality under such trying conditions. But his was a spirit not easily conquered, even by twenty years passed under a galling yoke. We have seen him descend meekly to the cellar, resigned to the dirty task of moving coal. But it must not be supposed that he did so with any sense of appropriateness or true humility. He lacked the coal-moving instinct. As he inserted the blade of the shovel, with a vicious push, into the pile of hard black lumps, his imagination was no less active than his arms.

"That for you!" he muttered. "That for you——" A grunt, and another savage lunge. "That for you, Maria Chidden, you domineerin' despot!"

Thirty minutes had passed in this manner, and a considerable hole had begun to appear in the black pile, when Mr. Chidden suddenly paused in the act of inserting the shovel, to consult a dollar nickel-plated watch in his pocket. Then, with the expression of one who has suddenly remembered something not unpleasant, he threw down the shovel, turned out the gas jet, mounted the stairs to the kitchen, crossed to the sink, and began washing his hands.

"Now what's the matter?" demanded Miss Chidden, entering from the dining room.

"I've got to go to the tailor for Mr. Stubbs' suit," replied Mr. Chidden calmly, feeling himself in a safe position.

"Humph!" grunted the lady. "It's a pity he don't go himself."

"Couldn't," said Mr. Chidden. "Sartorial wretchedness. He ain't got but one."

This argument being incontrovertible, Miss Chidden returned to the dining room without further comment. Mr. Chidden scrubbed his hands and face, put on a collar and tie and coat, and sought the street. Half a block to the east, he turned into the door of a basement shop, above which was a blackboard with the legend in gilt:

M. STURCKE,
Fine Tailoring
Gents' Suits Sponged and Pressed 50c.

"Morning," said Mr. Chidden, entering.

Two persons were in the shop—a fair-haired little woman with laughing blue eyes and an air of cheery amiability, and a young man with black hair and a pale, tragic countenance, who was energetically pounding on a tailor's goose with a heavy iron. The woman, laying aside a piece of cloth on which she was sewing, rose to greet the newcomer.

"Good morning, Mr. Chidden."

The caller, suddenly remembering his manners, jerked off his hat before he spoke:

"Very fine, Mrs. Sturcke. Out for a little breath of air. By the way, you have a suit—belongs to one of the roomers——"

"You want Mr. Stubbs' suit, yes? Leo, is the gray suit done?"

"In a minute," replied the pale-faced young man, and began to pound with the iron harder than ever.

"I'll wait," said Mr. Chidden, leaning himself gracefully against the counter.

Mrs. Sturcke resumed her chair and took up her work. The pale-faced young man glanced twice at the pair, and each time the iron came down with a fearful thud.

"How's business?" asked Mr. Chidden, with a professional air.

"Business is good," replied Mrs. Sturcke, in a tone which implied that nothing else was.

"It appears so," said Mr. Chidden, glancing knowingly at the row of coats and trousers hanging on the rail in the rear. "You've done admirable here, Mrs. Sturcke."

"As well as could be expected," agreed the lady.

"Yes, you have indeed. It's really surprising. As I said to Maria when your husband died two years ago, 'Women ain't tailors. She'll cavort.' But you haven't."

"No, I aind't." Mrs. Sturcke smiled. "But, of course, Miss Chidden—your sister—knew better yet. Not but what it's been hard. It's hard, anyway, being a widow."

Mr. Chidden shook his head sympathetically. "I know. Lonesome memories. Past illusions. I have 'em myself, though I must say I ain't a widow." Mr. Chidden sighed. "The fact is, I've never been married."

Mrs. Sturcke had begun to smile at his little joke about

not being a widow, but this last statement sobered her instantly.

"And that's a pity," she observed gravely. "It's not right, Mr. Chidden."

"Right!" exclaimed Mr. Chidden, with sudden energy. "Of course not! It's a fault! I admit it; it's a fault! But it's not mine. It takes two to make a bargain, Mrs. Sturcke, and I've never found the coequal."

"Some women is fools," declared Mrs. Sturcke emphatically.

"Here's the suit," the pale-faced young man broke in, glancing from one to the other.

Mr. Chidden took the suit and placed it over his arm—with the trousers underneath so the suspenders wouldn't show—and prepared to leave. Mrs. Sturcke helped him with the adjustment.

"Thanks," said Mr. Chidden courteously. "Good morning, ma'am."

There was a little, perplexed frown on Mr. Chidden's brow as he turned down Twenty-third Street, a frown that alternated, now with a smile, now with a whistle. When he reached the steps of the rooming house, the smile was in the ascendant, but as he entered the door the frown returned.

"I wonder," he said musingly to himself, "what the little widow meant by that about women being fools."

Then back came the smile, indicating, perhaps, that he had answered the question to his complete satisfaction.

By twelve o'clock the coal was moved to the last shining lump, and Mr. Chidden went to the kitchen to wash up. Throughout that operation he whistled—there was no tune to it, but he whistled—and his sister Maria, hearing it, looked across at him suspiciously.

"Robert," she exclaimed, "for goodness' sake stop that noise!"

He returned her gaze with an air of the utmost cheerfulness, threw the towel on a nail, and wandered into the back court.

After lunch, which he ate in the kitchen with his sister and the cook to avoid messing up the dining room, Mr. Chidden prepared to go out. This hour, from one to two, was his to do with as he liked, and he usually took advantage of the opportunity to walk down to the river, where he would loiter around watching the ferryboat crowds and the wagons of merchandise. For years he had been on friendly terms with the cabbies of the neighborhood, but the advent of taxis had thinned their ranks, and most of the old faces were gone.

On this day Mr. Chidden somehow did not feel like walking to the river.

"Sentiment of unrest," he muttered to himself, taking down an old brown slouch hat from a hook in the basement hall. He put the hat on his head, then suddenly snatched it off again, and stood gazing at it in quick fury. The next moment he started up the stairs with a firm and resolute step, down the hall and into the parlor, where his sister was removing the summer covers from the furniture.

"Well," said Miss Chidden, without looking up, "what are you fooling around here for? Remember, you get back by two o'clock. There's some rugs to beat."

"Maria," said Mr. Chidden calmly, "I want two dollars."

At that she did look up.

"What for?" she demanded in amazement.

"For a new hat. Look at that!" said Mr. Chidden, holding up the old brown slouch. "It's a disgrace. And, what's more, it don't fit, and it knows it. It's even ashamed of itself."

"That's all right," replied the lady accusingly, "but you bought it new last year."

But Mr. Chidden was in no mood for argument. He threw the hat on the floor with a gesture of scorn, and put his foot on it.

"Maria," he said coldly, "I asked you for two dollars."

"And I said," retorted his sister, "or at least I say, which is the same thing, that you shan't have it. Don't try to bully me, Robert Chidden. I won't stand it. Don't abuse your own sister. You can either wear that hat or go without. Pick it up!"

"Maria——"

"Robert!"

Mr. Chidden surrendered before the gleam of her eye. Fool that he had been, ever to have imagined he could conquer that steely glance! He picked up the hat, walked slowly to the hall, opened the door, and descended the steps to the street.

There he paused, undecided which way to turn. Certainly he did not want to walk to the river. The thing he would have liked most to do was to fight someone, pull his hair, kick him, punch his face; but that, he acknowledged to himself, was an impractical desire. He was a small man physically. He pulled the hat over his head, sighed heavily, and turned down the street to the right.

He walked slowly, aimlessly, with his hands thrust deep in his pockets and his shoulders stooped in dejection.

"Domineerin' despot!" he muttered aloud. "A man as is a man wouldn't stand it. Bob Chidden, you're a sexual disgrace."

These and other sundry self-accusations occupied his thoughts till he had nearly reached the end of the block. Suddenly he stopped and turned. Before him was a window bearing the inscription:

M. STURCKE,
Fine Tailoring
Gents' Suits Sponged and Pressed 50c.

For a minute Mr. Chidden stood and stared at the window, while his face gradually lost its gloom and became luminous with the brilliance of an idea. He took his hands from his pockets, removed the brown slouch hat, and pulled it into some sort of shape.

"My foot!" he exclaimed to himself, as if dazed by the temerity of his own conception. "My foot!"

Then suddenly his eyes brightened with the fire of determination. He pressed his lips firmly together, stepped down to the door of the tailor shop and opened it with a resolute hand.

"Good afternoon," said Mrs. Sturcke, looking up from her sewing as he entered.

"How de do, ma'am?" Mr. Chidden, glancing hastily around, observed with relief that the pale-faced young man was not in sight. "Out for a breath of air," he added, leaning against the counter and looking down at the plump little widow from the corner of one eye.

Mrs. Sturcke smiled pleasantly.

"I'm glad to know you can enjoy it, Mr. Chidden. For me, I don't ever seem to get the time. More work every day, though I suppose I shouldn't complain about that yet."

Mr. Chidden agreed that it was a good thing to have work to do, but hastened to add that it was a great pity that ladies should have no time for recreation.

"Walking," he declared, "is one of the great pleasures of life. It takes you away from things."

At this the widow smiled again, and invited Mr. Chidden to be seated. There were two empty chairs in the shop—one near the outer door, two paces from where he stood, and the other behind the counter, near that occupied by Mrs. Sturcke. Mr. Chidden hesitated a moment, then deliberately walked through the aisle to the other side of the counter and seated himself on the second chair.

This was, in fact, an amazing performance. In all the years that Mr. Chidden had been sitting down in the tailor shop, whether to wait for a suit of clothes or merely to chat, he had never chosen any other chair than the one by the outer door. It would appear that Mrs. Sturcke appreciated the significance of his action, for she colored visibly and bent a little closer over her sewing. Mr. Chidden himself appeared to be somewhat embarrassed. He took off his hat and put it on again, then removed it once more and dropped it on the floor.

"Don't do that, Mr. Chidden," said the widow, picking up the hat and placing it on the counter. "It'll get all soiled."

"Not it," said Mr. Chidden gloomily, his thoughts reverting to the late unpleasantness with his sister. Then he added hastily: "It's a bit off in color, but it's my favorite hat."

"Quite right, too," Mrs. Sturcke assented somewhat vaguely. "I like to see a man make his choice and stick to it. That was my husband's fault; he never knew what he wanted. Why, if you'd believe me, Mr. Chidden, he'd have some kind of newfangled thing in here every week. Otherwise he would have done well by the business, for he was a good worker."

"Still, he left you pretty well fixed," observed Mr. Chidden, glancing round the neat, well-kept shop.

Mrs. Sturcke stared at him as if surprised.

"As to that," she said finally, "you know well enough how I'm fixed, and your sister does, too. Not that I've anything to complain of Miss Chidden."

"It would be a wonder if you hadn't," returned Mr. Chidden, not quite understanding the widow's reference to his sister. Nor did he care to discuss so unpleasant a topic. "I tell you what, ma'am," he continued, throwing one leg over the other and sliding forward in his chair, "I have just about decided to leave my sister for good."

"You don't say so!" exclaimed Mrs. Sturcke, stopping her sewing to look at him.

"I do say so," declared Mr. Chidden almost fiercely. "Shall I tell you the truth, ma'am? I am not happy. I am becoming melancholy. Lonely aspirations. I shall leave and go far away."

"But where would you go?" cried the widow in evident eagerness. In her tone was admiration of the man's daring, and a note of something else—was it disappointment?

"I don't know," rejoined Mr. Chidden somberly. "But what does it matter, so long as I leave this life behind me? What does——"

"Mr. Chidden!" the widow interrupted in a voice of horror. "You wouldn't—you wouldn't—make away with yourself?"

Mr. Chidden stared at her blankly for a moment; then his face suddenly filled with comprehension.

"You misunderstand me," he explained. "Still, I have had the thought. There are some things, ma'am, that are more than enough to drive a man to suicide. A great sorrow—unguarded affections—only to be met with heartlessness and cruelty——" Mr. Chidden paused, overcome with feeling.

"It's a woman!" cried Mrs. Sturcke, dropping the sewing to the floor in her excitement.

"It is," agreed Mr. Chidden sadly. "But not my sister," he added hastily. "Not her. This woman—this heartless creature—is not like my sister. She is beautiful. She is a widow. She is far too beautiful for sanguinary hopes. And now you know who she is."

"I do not," declared Mrs. Sturcke. But her voice trembled, and her eyes were downcast.

"Then must I pronounce her name?" demanded Mr. Chidden, who was now pretty well worked up. "You will laugh at me, ma'am. Very well. I cannot control my affections. Unhappy passion! Mrs. Sturcke, the woman is you!"

Never was amorous avowal better delivered, nor with more telling effect. The widow's face grew red to her throat and ears. She kept her eyes on the floor, after one fleeting glance at the eager face of the impetuous lover.

"I don't know what you mean, Mr. Chidden," she said finally. But, hearing the tremble in her voice, Mr. Chidden cocked one eye—is it possible that he was winking to himself?—and leaned forward in his chair. His expression of hopeless despair gave way to an air of jaunty confidence; he reached forward and took the widow's hand in his own, and held it tight.

"Mrs. Sturcke—Gretta," he demanded in a voice vibrant with emotion, "am I to suffer longer?"

The widow raised her head, and turned beaming eyes to his.

"I'm sure I don't want you to suffer," she declared tremulously. "But, Mr. Chidden—are you sure yet—iss it me?"

Mr. Chidden masterfully took possession of the other hand. "Gretta, dear," he murmured, "Gretta, call me Robert."

"Well—Robert——"

"Will you marry me, Gretta?"

"Ach!"

Then and there was Mr. Bob Chidden like to have been smothered beneath the caresses of a transport of ecstasy. He was in fact bewildered and astonished, for though he had received more than one amiable smile from the plump little widow, he had not supposed that so violent a passion could have been aroused in her white bosom. It was an ordeal he had not counted on, and he might have been smothered literally but for the timely appearance of the pale-faced young man with the tragic eyes, who stopped short on the threshold at the sight that met his astonished gaze.

"Look out—it iss Leo!" cried the widow, tearing herself loose and retreating to her own chair.

The pale-faced young man passed through the shop to the room in the rear without speaking.

"Come back tonight," whispered Mrs. Sturcke softly. "He goes home at six o'clock."

"Tonight at seven. Darling! Happy love!" returned Mr.

Chidden, pressing her hand. "You will be waiting for me?"

"Yess, Robert."

Mr. Chidden emerged into the sunshine of Twenty-third Street with a springy, youthful step and a heart bounding with happiness. His hat was placed at a perilous angle on one side of his head, his hands were thrust deep in his pockets, and his shoulders swayed from side to side as he walked.

At last freedom! The twenty years' tyranny was at an end.

What a pleasant place that little shop was, to be sure! Of course, it wasn't worth much—perhaps six or eight hundred—but the custom was very good. It was two years now since Sturcke had died, and his widow had begun to run the place alone; it really wouldn't be surprising if she had managed to save up a thousand dollars. Just the right amount to put in a little stock of gents' furnishings—nothing elaborate, of course.

Suddenly Mr. Chidden stopped and swore at himself. As if it mattered whether the widow had saved up a thousand dollars or a thousand cents! As if it were not enough, and more than enough, that he was at last to escape from the inexorable clutches of his sister Maria! Never again to hear that hated voice raised in command! The joyousness of the thought caused Mr. Chidden to dance about on the sidewalk. He declared to himself that it would be worth it, even if he had to fire Leo and do all the work himself. At least, he would be master. He was humming a little tune under his breath as he turned in at the door of the rooming house.

"Robert!" came his sister's voice from the kitchen as he entered the hall.

Mr. Chidden descended the stairs with the step of a conqueror, flung the kitchen door open, and stood on the threshold.

"Well?" he inquired insolently.

His sister looked up from a pot she was stirring on the stove, and grunted.

"So you're back," she observed. "It's time. I want you to beat them rugs."

"All right," said Mr. Chidden cheerfully.

He went to the closet in the back hall, took therefrom the carpet beater, and returned to the kitchen. For some time he stood in the middle of the room, regarding his sister's back as she bent over the pot. His expression was an indescribable mixture of triumph and impudence.

"I'll clean 'em good," he observed finally, whirling the carpet beater about in the air, "because I may not get another chance at 'em."

"Now what are you talking about?" came from the pot.

"I say, I may not get another chance at the rugs, because I'm going to leave."

His sister turned to look at him.

"Leave! Leave where?"

"Leave here. This house. I'm going away, Maria."

But Maria refused to be at all impressed by this startling information.

"I suppose John D. has given you a million to start in business with," she observed sarcastically. "Now, you stop talking nonsense and do what I told you. And I don't want you running off a day or a week, either. I thought you was done with that foolishness. If you do, I won't let you in when you come back."

"Don't *you* worry," retorted Mr. Chidden. "I won't come back. It's different this time. The fact is, as you might say, I'm going to get married."

His sister whirled around, dropping the spoon in the pot with a splash.

"Married! You!" she exclaimed in a tone of scornful disbelief.

"Yes, married—me!" repeated Mr. Chidden warmly. "Married in every sense of the world. Just because you don't appreciate your own brother, Maria Chidden, is no sign some others wouldn't. It's a little love affair I run into. Amorous passion, my dear. She's a widow—remarkably beautiful woman—about half as old as you, I should say. Modern romance. *I* can't help it."

"Half as old as me! Romance!" cried Miss Maria shrilly, her face flaming, and trembling all over with anger. "Half as old as me, indeed!" she repeated. "Thank *you*, Robert Chidden!" She stopped a moment, choking with indignation; then demanded sternly: "Who is this woman?"

"You'd like to know, wouldn't you?" observed Mr. Chidden impudently.

"Yes, and what's more, I'm going to know."

"Maybe." Mr. Chidden threw the carpet beater over his shoulder and started for the door. "She's a lady, and she's a widow, and that's all I have to say," he threw back.

Silence pursued him to the door and a few paces into the court. He had flung four rugs over the line and was picking up the fifth when his sister's voice, sharp, with a ring in it, came from the kitchen:

"Robert! Is it Gretta Sturcke?"

Mr. Chidden returned to the door, and stood looking in.

"If it is," he replied truculently, "what about it?"

Then he became silent with wonder at the change that took place in his sister's face. Her eyes, which had glared with indignation, lost their fire and assumed their normal expression of calm and relentless tyranny; her lips were pressed together in a grim smile of satisfaction; the red flag of agitated displeasure disappeared from her cheeks. Mr. Chidden's brain entertained the astounding idea that his sister Maria was actually pleased by the information that he was to marry Gretta Sturcke!

"What—what is it?" he faltered at last. "What's the matter?"

"Matter? Nothing!" Miss Chidden chuckled. "So she

got you, did she? I suppose she thinks I'll make a fool of myself. Well, I won't. What I've got, I'll keep. Though, to be sure, I shan't be sorry to have you around the shop; goodness knows you're no account here. And it'll save me Leo's wages, as soon as you learn to do the work."

These words were Greek to Mr. Chidden, but he felt somehow that they were ominous. Why should his sister Maria pay Leo's wages? Why——He felt himself grow pale as a horrible thought entered his mind. Could it be possible? Could fate play him so dastardly a trick?

"Maria," he stammered, "what do you mean?"

Again Miss Chidden chuckled.

"Ask Gretta Sturcke," she advised sardonically. "Ask her why she wants a little spindle-legged thing like you for a husband. Lord knows she didn't have much luck with the first one. If it hadn't been for me stepping in when he died and paying eight hundred dollars for a business that wasn't worth a cent more than seven hundred and fifty, she'd have found herself without a roof over her head. And besides that, I gave her a job to live on. Ain't I been payin' her twelve dollars a week just to look after the place? Lord knows it ain't made me rich, but I haven't lost anything, and with you there, Robert, to watch things, and me to watch you, I guess it won't be so bad. Only I have to laugh at Gretta Sturcke. I suppose she thought I'd give you the shop for a wedding present. Humph!"

Mr. Chidden gasped, tottered, and sank into a chair.

"Maria," he said weakly, "do you mean to say that tailor shop is *yours?*"

"I do," answered Miss Chidden dryly. "Can't you understand plain English? Romance! Huh! You're a fine subject for romance, you are! Go on out and beat them rugs."

ART FOR ART'S SAKE

Mr. Bob Chidden stood in the middle of the kitchen floor, completely surrounded by wastebaskets. On the coal range at his right an immense pot of stew was simmering reluctantly; in the left-hand corner, near the window, the kitchen girl was peeling potatoes, standing first on one foot, then on the other.

"Awful trash!" commented Mr. Chidden, with a gloomy and dejected air. Then, suddenly, precipitately he stooped over and picked up four of the wastebaskets, two in each hand. His sister Maria had entered from the dining room.

"A whole week!" said Miss Maria forcefully. "Crammed plumb full, every one of 'em. What are you standing there for? Mind what I say! After this you empty them wastebaskets every day, Robert Chidden!"

These last words were probably not heard by Mr. Chidden, who had disappeared hurriedly down the cellar steps with the four baskets. He emptied their contents into the furnace and returned for more. Then, the destructive portion of his menial task completed, he began to return the empty baskets to the rooms above—three on the first floor, four on the second, and three on the third. All of the rooms appeared to be empty save the third-floor front. At the door of this Mr. Chidden paused to knock.

"Your wastebasket, Mr. Glover," he called loudly.

"All right. Bring it in," came from the room.

Mr. Chidden entered.

To describe the room it is only necessary to say that it was like all others in an ordinary New York rooming house. The table near which Mr. Chidden set down the wastebasket was of imitation mahogany, soiled with water stains and covered with scars. The bed at which he glanced as he straightened up was made of iron that had once been painted white, with brass knobs at the corners. The man in the bed, dressed in yellow pajamas with pink stripes, was a tousle-haired, sleepy-eyed young fellow of twenty-six or seven, with regular features and an amiable countenance.

"What time is it?" demanded this personage, yawning.

Mr. Chidden replied that it was about eleven o'clock, and moved toward the bed, while an expression of envy disturbed the settled melancholy of his face. He could not remember a single occasion when he had been permitted to remain in bed till eleven o'clock, whereas Mr. Glover enjoyed that blissful privilege seven days in the week.

"It's a fine thing, being at the theater," said Mr. Chidden abruptly, blinking over the iron foot rail.

Mr. Glover kicked the sheets to one side, sat up, yawned, twisted himself slowly around, and placed his bare feet on the floor.

"Not on your life!" he returned amiably, reaching for a garment on the back of a chair. "It's hard work. What makes you think it's fine?"

Mr. Chidden grunted.

"Eleven o'clock, and you just getting up. Ain't that enough?"

"Oh, if it comes to that," returned Mr. Glover carelessly, "it strikes me that you have it pretty soft yourself, Chidden. Regular snap, I'd call it."

"What? Me?" gasped Mr. Chidden.

The other nodded, standing up to pull on his trousers.

"Me!" Mr. Chidden gasped again incredulously. "I'm surprised, Mr. Glover, since my sister is known to you. My position is chronical. I get up at five o'clock in the morning for the furnace. And from then till night not a minute is my own—not a minute! Regular snap! It's a cursed existence such as no man should submit to. For twenty years I've been smothered—smothered under a woman's skirts—my own sister's!" He paused a moment for breath, then muttered, as if to himself, half savagely, half morosely: "Miserable slave!"

"You surprise me," observed Mr. Glover, from the washbasin. "I thought you had a pretty easy time of it, Chidden. Plenty to eat, not much of anything to do, no rent to worry about, no——"

"And when I want a new hat, I go and beg Maria for a dollar and fifty cents," put in Mr. Chidden bitterly.

"Well, you get it."

"Not always. Stringy finance, she says. I've never talked like this to any one before, but let me tell you one thing, Mr. Glover: The underwear on me at this moment is some that my sister Maria bought for herself and couldn't wear because it scratched. It's big in front—you know—and it's embroidered at the neck. I cut the legs off. It's a union suit."

"My God!" exclaimed Mr. Glover, with a shout of laughter. "I'd like to see it, Chidden—I would, indeed! It must be a rare sight."

"No, you wouldn't. I can't bear to look at it myself. I shut my eyes when I put it on."

"Why don't you get a job?" Mr. Glover was still laughing as he stood before the mirror adjusting his tie.

"I have. Many of 'em. But it's no go. It's fate. I was a

merchant once, you know—had a shop up in New Rochelle. Forced out and had to come here. If I get a job, it's no good."

Mr. Chidden sighed, turning toward the door. He had nearly reached it when he was halted abruptly by the voice of Mr. Glover.

"I might find something for you at the theater," said the actor.

Mr. Chidden stood with his mouth open and his hand on the doorknob. He seemed amazed.

"At the theater!" he stammered finally. "You don't mean—on the stage?"

"Well, hardly," smiled the other. "Something—let's see—say, claquer, for instance." He pronounced it "clacker." "Burrie has a première on Thursday, and he'll probably need 'em. I hear it's a rotten show—nothing to it except the courtroom scene and a bit of character done by a friend of mine. Something in my line, I believe. Pretty fat—sure to get a hand."

"What's a clacker?" inquired Mr. Chidden, having waited impatiently for the other to finish.

The actor explained:

"A come-on guy for the audience—to start the applause and keep it up. The theaters all have 'em, more or less."

"Could you—do you think——" stammered Mr. Chidden, his face pale with hope.

"Sure! At least I think so. It means fifty cents or a dollar a night, a little spending money—and, besides, you get to see the show. I'll see Burrie this afternoon at rehearsal and let you know in the morning."

Mr. Chidden's outburst of profuse thanks was interrupted by a sound that came from below—the sound of a rasping, strident voice calling a name. He hurriedly opened the door, and the voice became distinct:

"Robert!"

"It's Maria," said Mr. Chidden, gritting his teeth. "She

wants me to sweep the sidewalk. If you'd be so kind, Mr. Glover——"

"Sure!" returned the actor. "Run along, Chidden. See you tomorrow."

II.

About ten o'clock of the following Thursday morning, Mr. Chidden opened the door and stepped into the parlor, where his sister Maria was dusting bric-a-brac—a task she never entrusted to servants. At sound of her brother's entrance, she stood up and turned to look at him.

"Well?" she observed truculently.

"I just wanted to tell you," said Mr. Chidden, standing by the door, "that I've got a job."

His sister snorted contemptuously, and was silent, awaiting details.

"It's a night job at the theater," the little man continued. "Mr. Glover recommended me. A sort of critic, you might say. I won't be home till midnight, so you'd better have Annie tend to the furnace in the morning. I saw Mr. Burrie, the manager, yesterday. At the Columbus. Probably I'll be working for him all winter." Mr. Chidden paused and turned, with his hand on the knob. "Dramatic triumph," he announced firmly, in a loud tone, and then went out, closing the door with a bang behind him.

He felt uplifted, elated, for several reasons. He knew that his sister was rather stunned, though she wouldn't show it. That was delightful in itself. Then he was about to earn a dollar—many of them. He had figured it all up. The theatrical season would be about thirteen weeks. Averaging four nights a week, that would be one hundred and forty-four dollars. A new suit of clothes, a meerschaum pipe, a dozen ball games—in short, anything and everything. And he would have money to jingle in his pocket!

But what was perhaps best of all, he would go to the

best theaters free—many of them—all of them; for Burrie
had promised to use him at all his first nights as well as
at subsequent performances. Nothing could have pleased
Mr. Chidden better. If he could not properly be called a
student of the modern drama, it was only because he had
lacked opportunity for the collection of material. He had
never seen the interior of a Broadway theater. But he spent
twenty cents every night during the season at the stock
theater around the corner on Eighth Avenue, and he was
known to the delicatessen proprietor, tailor, cabmen, and
other gentlemen of the neighborhood as a man to whom
the deepest subtleties of the actor's art were an open book.

So he was overjoyed at this opportunity to behold a
Broadway star in a Broadway production. That he was
actually to be paid for his attendance appeared to him little
short of marvelous. He said to himself that there was no
other job in all the world that would have pleased him so
well as this one; and in order to make sure of giving
satisfaction to Mr. Burrie, he spent most of the afternoon
in the cellar, practicing the art of handclapping. For more
than an hour he sat on an old soap box near the furnace,
bringing his palms together, now with sharp, staccato reports, again with a measured, thunderous impact that
sounded like the discharge of a small cannon. After an
hour of experiment, he decided that the most effective
method was a mixture of the two, neither too fast nor too
loud, and with the hands hollowed but slightly. Satisfied,
he went to the kitchen to polish his shoes.

He arrived at the theater a little after eight, feeling that
it would not do to display any eagerness in the matter. He
would show them that he was an old hand at this theater
business. The lobby was filled with loungers, and Mr.
Chidden found some difficulty in making his way to the
brass rails that guarded the entrance to the auditorium.
There he presented the card Mr. Burrie had given him to
a fat, pompous personage who was mostly red face and
white shirt front.

Mr. Chidden spoke to him in a low and mysterious tone.

"From Mr. Burrie," said he. "I'm an official."

The other merely grunted and passed him in.

From the head usher Mr. Chidden learned that he was not to pursue his activities alone. That person, a tired-looking, wise-looking youth, informed him that his companion was already at the appointed spot, and called an usher to conduct Mr. Chidden thither. It proved to be a seat at the extreme right of the parquet, toward the rear.

"There he is, over the end," said the usher. "His name is Mintz. He'll tell you what to do. You should have come early so as not to disturb people."

Mr. Chidden smothered the retort that rose to his lips, edged his way through to the empty seat, sat down, and looked about him. The parquet was filled with men in evening dress and women with necks, of all ages and appearances. It was what the newspapers call a "typical first-night audience," but the sight was new to Mr. Chidden, and he spent several minutes studying it. Then he turned his attention to his neighbor and confrère on the right.

What he saw was a wrinkled, uneven countenance, decorated with a sandy mustache, reddish hair, and gray, slumberous eyes. Mr. Chidden had studied the profile for about a minute when he was startled by seeing the gray eyes turned directly upon him in a fixed, contemptuous gaze. The two men looked at each other for some seconds in a silence that was finally broken by Mr. Chidden.

"Is this Mr. Mintz?" he asked abruptly.

"Who are you?" inquired the other, more abruptly still, in a tone that held an indication of hostility.

"Chidden," replied our hero courteously. "From Mr. Burrie. I was told to take my orders from Mr. Mintz. I'm the new clacker."

"I'm Mintz," returned the other, apparently somewhat mollified. "That's me—Jake Mintz. You follow me. Clap when I do, and stop when I do. That's all. What do you get?"

"Why, I don't know—what do you mean?" stammered Mr. Chidden.

"What does Burrie pay you?"

"Oh, I see! You refer to the remunatory element. One dollar."

Mr. Mintz stared a moment, grunted twice, and turned his head back to its original position, facing the stage. It was evident that he considered the conversation finished. But Mr. Chidden had a dozen questions on the tip of his tongue, and had just opened his mouth for the first one when the lights were suddenly lowered and a hush fell over the audience. Glancing toward the stage, he saw the curtain slowly rising.

The first act Mr. Chidden regarded as rather slow. He got the impression of a lot of empty talk, but nothing happened. By the end of the act he had gathered a hazy idea that the man with the beard and the gray spats was trying to induce the wife of the little chap in the dressing gown to run away from her husband; but he was unable to decide whether the wife was the lady in the blue velvet suit with white furs or the one that lay on the divan smoking cigarettes with a cynical smile. Altogether it was disappointing; and, as the curtain fell, Mr. Chidden turned to his colleagues and said so.

"Shut up and clap!" returned Mr. Mintz, without glancing at him.

Mr. Chidden perceived that he was neglecting his duty. Anxious to make up for lost time, he brought the palms of his hands together with a succession of thunderous reports, forgetting, in his excitement, the results of his experiments in the cellar during the afternoon. He was brought up sharply by hearing Mr. Mintz growl in his ear:

"Not so loud, you boob!"

Mr. Chidden eased up a little, and continued with moderation. But when the tumult had died down and the curtain had fallen on the last recall, he leaned over and whispered, in a firm tone:

"I am not a boob, Mr. Mintz."

Mr. Mintz paid no attention whatever. He did not move his head; he did not utter a word. Mr. Chidden stared at him for a moment, then turned to the program, which occupied his time throughout the intermission.

The second act was better. The man with the beard and the gray spats started something at the very first by spiriting the lady in the blue velvet suit with white furs to a private room in a restaurant. At first the lady tried to escape, then she calmly sat down and fanned herself, evidently resolving to make the best of a disagreeable situation. Enter husband, through a French window. Small as he was, he appeared not at all frightened by the presence of the man with the beard. Instead he calmly asked his wife if she had finished her supper, offered his arm, and escorted her out. Mr. Chidden was rather of the opinion that the man with the beard should have been knocked down with a chair or something, but decided that it was perhaps just as well not. The instant the curtain began to fall, he burst out into loud applause, genuine and sustained.

"You began too soon," said Mr. Mintz, when the applause had died away.

"The sooner, the better," returned Mr. Chidden. "Enthusiasm, sir."

Mr. Mintz glared, while his whisper became a growl.

"I say you began too soon. After this wait for me."

Mr. Chidden had a mind to argue the question, but felt the futility of it and decided to hold his peace, observing to himself that it was quite evident that Mr. Mintz was totally lacking in the quality of artistic perception. He appeared to regard his position of claquer merely as a job, an ordinary and not too interesting means of making a dollar. Mr. Chidden glanced at him with a sort of pity.

"Brutish fellow!" he murmured under his breath. "Still, I suppose he needs the money."

These reflections occupied his mind till the beginning of the third act.

Mr. Chidden was looking forward to this third act with a pleasant sense of expectation. He was acquainted with the rules of drama as well as any other patron of the Eighth Avenue Stock Company, and he knew very well what was coming. This was the act in which the man with the beard and the gray spats should receive a tremendous jolt on the jaw delivered by the little chap in the dressing gown, who would then take his weeping wife in his arms and announce, in broken tones: "I forgive you, Nellie." These scenes always aroused the greatest enthusiasm in Mr. Chidden's breast, and he was looking forward to this one with keen relish.

The curtain rose, discovering the man with the beard lying in an easy-chair, reading and smoking. The door opened R. Entered the lady with the blue velvet suit with white furs. Breathing through her nose, she announced, in a trembling voice, that she had come—she couldn't stay away. The man with the beard arose and carelessly threw his arms around her and kissed her. Mr. Chidden trembled with indignation. He kissed her again.

The door opened L. Entered husband.

"Ah!" cried Mr. Chidden. "Now for it!"

Husband walked up to wife, whose face was white.

"Why are you here?" he asked.

"Because—I—love—him," she replied, clinging to the man with the beard.

"Oh, really?" said the husband. "Humph! Well, that makes a difference. All right, Nellie; suit yourself. By the way, Jones, old man, have you got a cigarette about?"

And this fiend of a husband got his cigarette, lit it, said farewell to his wife in a bored, careless tone, and departed. Then the other man turned and——

But Mr. Chidden could stand it no longer. Already he

was on his feet. His lips were parted, his teeth were set together, and from the instrument thus fashioned there came forth a sound as if gallons of water had been poured on a bed of red-hot coals. So superlative, so aggressive, so pronounced a hiss had never before been heard on Broadway. The entire audience turned from the stage and bestowed their attention on this critic from Eighth Avenue. Some laughed; others said, "Sh-sh-h!" in shocked tones; the remainder merely stared. Mr. Chidden felt someone pulling at his sleeve, and the voice of Mr. Mintz sounded in his ear:

"Sit down, you boob! Sit down!"

But Mr. Chidden, encouraged by opposition, like all brave and sincere men, only hissed the louder. Laughter was heard on all sides, punctuated by cries of "Shame!" "Put him out!" "Sit down!" Half the audience was on its feet, stretching necks to see. Somewhere to the left a woman screamed. Mr. Chidden was jerked back violently into his seat, and the voice of Mr. Mintz sounded in his ear:

"Cut it out, you boob!"

"I won't!" yelled Mr. Chidden furiously. "It's a rotten show, Mintz, and you know it! Let me go! Let me go!"

And once more Mr. Chidden began to hiss desperately, violently.

Then everything happened at once. The curtain was rung down. Ushers came leaping down the aisles. The theater was filled with a hubbub of laughter and shouts. It was a crisis, but Mr. Mintz proved himself equal to it. He placed his arms firmly around Mr. Chidden's waist, lifted his struggling form to his shoulders, pushed his way through to the aisle, and ran swiftly toward the entrance, with Mr. Chidden hissing all the way. He did not halt until he reached the outer door of the lobby, where he hurled his burden onto the sidewalk and stood panting for breath.

"Go on, you boob!" he called wrathfully. "Get out of here, you boob!"

Mr. Chidden slowly arose to his feet. Passersby had halted to stare curiously, but he paid no attention to them. For several seconds he stood regarding the entrance to the lobby with thoughtful seriousness, and now and then the soft suggestion of a hiss came from his lips. He even took a tentative step toward the blazing lights of the entrance, when suddenly the face of Mr. Burrie appeared just within the glass doors. Mr. Chidden hesitated, stopped, and turned.

"Rotten show!" he muttered gloomily, and moved away.

Twenty minutes later he had reached the rooming house and let himself in. All was dark and silent. He made his way up one, two, three flights, to a little room in the rear at the very top—a cold, bare, cheerless room. Slowly he undressed himself. Then, with a sigh, he reached for the alarm clock and set it for a quarter past five.

"Miserable slave!" murmured Mr. Chidden.

ANOTHER LITTLE
LOVE AFFAIR

M r. Chidden had not felt very well that morning. He thought it must be an attack of biliousness. Or was it merely an unusually acute stroke of the gloomy melancholy which he had acquired in twenty years of service as handyman in his sister's rooming house?

Not that he wasted any time arguing the matter with himself. He merely felt that he did not feel well. After breakfast, he had spent an hour sifting the ashes from the furnace. Then he had brought up coal for the kitchen range, swept off the stoop and sidewalk, set out the garbage and ash cans, shined the brass doorknobs and rail, and beat four rugs. These tasks completed, he went in search of his sister to ask for forty cents to buy gas mantles.

"She's upstairs, sewing," said Minnie, the kitchen girl.

Mr. Chidden mounted two flights and passed down the narrow hall to the rear end, where a door stood half open—the door to his sister's room. In front of it, he paused. There were two reasons for this. He always paused for courage when about to face his sister, even when his errand was perfectly disinterested; but this time his hesitation came partly from surprise. Why did he not hear the sewing machine, with its monotonous, aggressive whir? And whose was the voice—certainly not his sister's—whose unintelligible mumble came vaguely to his ears through the half-open door? Presumably it was someone talking to his sister. Who could it be? For two minutes Mr. Chidden stood motionless, listening and wondering.

And then suddenly came another sound, as the voice halted—the sound of a smacking kiss!

Mr. Chidden gasped with profound amazement. And before he could close his mouth again, he heard the sound of swift footsteps, the door was flung open from within, and a man rushed from the room, dashed to the stairs, and descended, two steps at a time. But, despite the rapidity of his flight, Mr. Chidden recognized him. It was Comicci, the Italian sculptor, who occupied a bedroom studio in the third-floor front.

Mr. Chidden stood for a moment struck dumb, then came to with a start as the street door banged below. Simultaneously came the whir of the sewing machine from within the room. He tiptoed to the stairs and began to descend noiselessly. On the fourth step, he halted and stood still, and finally he turned abruptly, remounted to the landing, walked briskly to the open door, and entered the room.

"Well?" said his sister, stopping the machine to look across at him.

Miss Maria Chidden was a raw-boned, red-faced woman of forty-two, with dim gray eyes, hard cheeks, and shiny skin. Particularly, her face was very red; but, as Mr. Chidden looked at her, after a quick glance around to see if she was alone, it appeared to him that her color was even higher than usual. This, and the fact that there was no one else in the room, pointed to a simple and certain conclusion. Mr. Comicci had kissed her, or attempted to kiss her. But it was inconceivable to Mr. Chidden that any man in the world, for any reason whatever, would kiss his sister Maria. He was as much puzzled as amazed.

"Well?" Miss Maria repeated impatiently.

"I want forty cents for gas mantles," said Mr. Chidden, from the middle of the room.

Without a word, she arose, unlocked a drawer of a dingy, old-fashioned desk, and took out a big black pocketbook. From this she extracted two quarters, which she handed to her brother. His amazement increased. Never before had she given him one cent over the exact amount required. She must be horribly agitated. She might even——

He cleared his throat, stuck the fifty cents into his pocket, and spoke:

"Also, I want three dollars."

Miss Chidden paused in the act of returning the pocketbook to the drawer.

"What for?" she demanded.

"For myself."

"What for?"

"Imperial necessity," said Mr. Chidden, trying to make a joke of it.

"I suppose it's clothes."

Her tone was maddening. The flush was leaving her face now, and her lips were straightening out. These ominous signs, and the smart sarcasm of her voice, plunged Mr. Chidden quite suddenly into the depths of exasperated despair. From her appearance of nervous embarrassment, he had thought to take her by surprise and get the three dollars out of her before she realized what she was doing. But he knew that hope was gone as he saw her lips meet in the familiar straight line. Very well, he would fight for it.

"Yes, it's clothes," he replied, with sudden passion. "Why shouldn't it be? I want three dollars."

"You can't have it." Miss Maria returned the pocketbook to the drawer. "And, what's more, you don't need it."

"No? I don't?" shouted Mr. Chidden, advancing a step and pointing indignantly to a certain portion of his clothing. "Look at that! Just look at it! Perhaps there is men who can wear a pair of pants three years, Maria Chidden, but I'm not one of 'em. It's unwholesome. Give me three dollars."

For reply, Miss Maria closed and locked the drawer, returned to her chair, inserted the edge of a sheet under the hemmer, and started the machine. Her only audible comment was a grunt as she hitched the chair up closer.

Mr. Chidden choked with the helpless rage of the timid and oppressed.

"That's right!" he yelled. "Shut your mouth and look mad. You can't scare me. I need a pair of pants, and you know it. You ought to be ashamed of yourself. You've got rich off of this boarding house, and I've slaved for you morning, noon and night for twenty years, and got nothing. What's three dollars to you? Anyway, I've got it coming to me. I've earned it. Ain't I? Haven't I earned it?"

"Maybe," was the calm reply. "But you're not going to get it."

"No? I won't get it? All right! All right, then, I won't get it!"

And Mr. Chidden, tasting defeat, sought for revenge. He tried to think of something to say that would give this tyrant pain. And what he found was:

"What was that little dago doing in here? I saw him come out."

The machine stopped. Miss Maria arose. Her look was awful. Mr. Chidden met it bravely for three seconds, then began a precipitate retreat toward the door. He was halted by her voice. Anyone would have been.

"Robert!"

"Well?" he murmured, turning.

"Let me tell you right now, Mr. Comicci is no dago. He's a gentleman. Dago, indeed! A worthless little thing like you to call him names! And you stand right up and insinuate your own sister! Yes, you did! And if ever I—— Robert! Robert, come back here!"

But the call went unheeded. With his revenge, Mr. Chidden had swiftly flown—into the hall and down three flights of stairs to the cellar. There he halted and seated himself on an old box behind the coal pile. Almost immediately he jumped up again, ran to the cellar door, and bolted it. Then he returned to the box. This was the refuge he always sought when he required solitude. He took a pipe from his pocket, filled it, lit it, and leaned back against the whitewashed wall to puff and think.

First, he thought of pants. For two weeks now he had been screwing up his courage to the point of asking for three dollars—the price of a certain handsome garment displayed in Greenberg's window on Eighth Avenue. And since his need was undeniable, he knew that if he had approached his sister in the proper manner, with a due amount of humility and appeal, he would have been successful. But he had allowed himself to be betrayed by a hasty impulse, and now he would probably have to wait another month.

What had set him off? Oh, yes, the dago. That was funny. Of course he had been mistaken; even a dago would not make love to his sister Maria, who was lean and old and rawboned. But then he had distinctly heard the kiss. What if it had really happened? Mr. Chidden puffed out a long column of smoke, and chuckled to himself. He would give anything to have seen the little dago trying to kiss Maria. For some time he sat smoking and grinning to himself, developing many amusing details of the imagined scene.

Then suddenly he sat up with a quick ejaculation, jerking the pipe from his mouth. By Heaven! He hadn't thought of that! Could it be? Perhaps the little dago wasn't such a fool, after all!

He leaned back against the wall and began to think in earnest, forgetting to smoke. He remained thus for half an hour, silent, motionless, rapt. Then he slowly arose, knocked the ashes from his pipe, and went upstairs to look at the dining-room clock. It said a quarter past eleven, which meant that Miss Maria had left fifteen minutes before on her daily trip to the Eighth Avenue markets.

"Now's my chance!" muttered Mr. Chidden.

He mounted to the second floor and passed to the rear of the hall. The door, behind which he had heard the kiss an hour before, was closed. Getting no answer to his knock, he pushed it open and entered. Leaving the door ajar, he tiptoed across to the old-fashioned desk and raised the lid, disclosing to view an orderly heap of receipts, bills, and other papers, and two medium-sized books bound in imitation leather. He took out one of the latter, laid it on the desk, and opened it.

He was nervous; he kept glancing behind him every second, and his fingers trembled, but he finally found what he wanted on page 47. At the top of the leaf was written: "Giacomo Comicci, came in Sept. 22, third-floor front, $5.00." Beneath this was a list of dates a week apart, and after each date appeared the entry: "Paid $5.00." But at March 16th the entries of payments halted, though the dates continued. Mr. Chidden glanced at the calendar on the desk, which displayed in black type: "June 28." Then he went down the line of dates with his finger, counting.

"By Polly!" he exclaimed aloud, for getting the danger of his situation. "He hasn't paid a cent for fifteen weeks!"

All was clear. His suspicions were justified. No wonder the little dago was trying to kiss Maria! Then another thought came: Never before had any roomer succeeded in remaining under Maria's roof for more than three consecutive weeks without paying rent, and here—nearly four months! Gradually, reluctantly, Mr. Chidden arrived at the painful conclusion that not only had Mr. Comicci given Maria the kiss, but also that she had been glad to get it.

But he knew his sister Maria. She was a prude if ever there was one. No man—not Don Juan himself—could ever have succeeded in planting the salute of love on her chaste cheek without having first declared the most honorable intentions. By Polly! There could be no doubt of it! The little dago was trying to marry Maria!

Mr. Chidden was thinking fast, but it was some time later, back in the cellar, that he arrived at this startling conclusion. As soon as it entered his mind, it crowded everything else out. He felt himself suddenly confronted by a fearful and wholly unexpected danger. His brain whirled.

True, he had told himself daily for the past twenty years that he was living the life of a slave, and he had made spasmodic and energetic, but fruitless, attempts to get out of it. Handyman in a rooming house is not a position either of honor or of ease, and his sister Maria had taken all the profits. But still the work was not really hard, he never had to worry about anything, he usually got clothes when he had to have them, and he could always squeeze a little spending money out of Maria when his need was urgent. And Maria had saved up something like ten thousand dollars. Not that he wanted or expected her to die, or anything like that; but the fact remained that the ten thousand existed, and that he was her brother, her only living relative.

And now this little dago——

About the middle of the afternoon, Mr. Chidden mounted to the third floor and knocked on the door at the front. His was no coward spirit. He had no special design or object; he merely wanted to face the enemy and appraise him. Signor Comicci opened the door.

"I've come to see to the gas," said Mr. Chidden, entering.

"There is nothing wronga weeth eet," answered the Italian.

Without bothering to reply, Mr. Chidden got a chair from a corner and carried it to the middle of the floor under the chandelier; then, mounting on it, he proceeded to examine the top of the burner with a singular expression of hostility, due, perhaps, to the fact that every now and then his eyes shifted for a quick glance at the Italian, who stood beside the chair looking up curiously. The look was curious, and nothing more; there was certainly nothing vicious in the face, with its twinkling gray eyes beneath the straggling brown hair. But Mr. Chidden found it evil; and he was on the point of making an ill-natured remark, when it occurred to him that, in the role of spy, it is necessary to submerge the violent emotions.

"I guess it's all right," he said finally, descending from the chair.

Mr. Comicci nodded amiably.

"Gives trouble sometimes," continued Mr. Chidden. "On account of the mantle. Jets is easy. But I suppose a good light."

Thus the conversation began; and, despite a certain wary hesitancy of manner, Mr. Comicci entered into it with zest and affability. Within three minutes he was telling of his sorrow at having been compelled to give up his studio on Tenth Street, declaring that overhead light was essential to his art; after which he discoursed for some time on the stony path of the artist, especially the artist in marble and bronze.

"So costly the material!" he complained, while Mr. Chidden nodded in the effort to appear sympathetic. "Look at this! Just the marble, eet costa five dollar!"

He indicated a figure group, a boy sitting on a man's knee, half-finished. Mr. Chidden displayed a diplomatic interest, eyeing the group with the air of a man who un-

derstands more than he is willing to admit. He had to pay
for the pretense. From that figure they passed to another,
and another. The room was full of them—just begun, half
finished, and completed. The Italian dragged them from
all sorts of places—a leaping frog in bronze from under
a heap of sketches, a boy with a flute from a soiled laun-
dry bag, a girl poring over a book from a drawer of the
wardrobe.

"I show you something," he said suddenly, going to a
corner where stood a table with something on it covered
with a dark cloth. "Eet has been at Demarest in exhibit.
Only yesterday eet came back. I did eet long ago—so
beautiful—see!"

He carefully removed the dark cloth, displaying the figure of a woman in white marble. There was no drapery.
Her arms were crossed on her breast, and one knee was
bent a little inward; her head was half turned, as if in
shamed modesty. It *was* beautiful.

"By Polly!" exclaimed Mr. Chidden, after a minute's
critical survey; and then he added thoughtfully: "Bare as
a picked chicken."

It was the sight of that nude figure that gave Mr. Chidden his idea. But it came later—three or four days later—
for in the presence of the figure he was really somewhat
abashed. And the seed of Mr. Chidden's strategy was the
muttering to himself as he went downstairs after leaving
Mr. Comicci:

"I'd like to see Maria's face when she looked at *that!*"

The immediate effect of his visit was to soften his suspicion of Mr. Comicci. He seemed so harmless and amiable, and, poor devil that he was, what did it matter if he
beat Maria out of some rent? Mr. Chidden was only too
glad to see his sister done for once. He began to doubt if
the kiss had really been delivered; and, looking at Maria's
face, he strongly doubted if any man, in any extremity,
would have the temerity to kiss her.

It was about a week later that his doubts vanished de-

cidedly and suddenly. Coming through the hall one afternoon, he heard an indistinct murmur of voices behind the
closed door of the parlor. As his footsteps approached,
the voices became silent; but as he reached the top of the
stairs on the floor above, they came again to his ears, very
faintly. Instantly he was suspicious. He halted, and stood
still to think, with a hesitation born not of any scruples
of morality, but to bolster up his courage. Then he returned to the stairs and descended slowly, noiselessly.
From the hall the voices were audible, but he could not
catch the words. He tiptoed cautiously to the door of the
library in the rear and across to the curtains that hung
between that room and the parlor, and, with a beating
heart and set lips, he peeped through their folds.

What he saw was his sister Maria seated on the green
plush sofa, her face redder than ever, and an absurd ten-
derness in her eyes, gazing fondly at Mr. Comicci, who
was kneeling on the carpet at her feet and holding fast to
both her hands!

The Italian's voice came, plainly audible.

"You will! You will!" he murmured passionately.

He began to plant furious kisses all over her hands. She
shook her head.

"I'm too old. You can't love me," the astonished Mr.
Chidden heard her say.

"Ah!" groaned the lover. "Ah, what is age when one is
beautiful? So beautiful! Eet is to break my heart!"

Still she shook her head, but with less determination. It
was easy to see that she was yielding. The ardent wooer
took one knee from the floor, passed an arm around her
waist, and resumed the hand-kissing.

"So beautiful and pure!" he cried in an exalted whisper.
It was wonderful. No one but a Latin could possibly have
done it. "I implore you—ah—make me happy! Be my
wife!"

And then came the voice of Minnie, the kitchen girl,
from below:

"Mr. Chidden! Mr. Chid-*den!*"

Mr. Chidden, with an inward curse, turned so quickly that he nearly betrayed himself by knocking over a lamp pedestal. The voice of Minnie continued, rising higher. He tiptoed silently into the hall and down the stairs, meeting Minnie at the foot.

"What the heck do you want?" he demanded savagely.

"The man's here for the bottles," she replied in a tone of surprise at his manner of unaccustomed violence.

After all, as he told himself when he had retired to the cellar that evening to think, the interruption was of little consequence. He had seen and heard enough. Whether Maria had said yes or no, it was certain that she would eventually say yes.

"Indecent amorosity!" said Mr. Chidden aloud.

He sat down and began to think.

And fate played into his hands. The scheme was his own, but opportunity came from Maria herself. It was the next morning when she called him upstairs to order him to beat the parlor rugs and lay a fire in the grate. This in preparation for a meeting of the Help a Little Club, to be held on Thursday.

It was not the first time Mr. Chidden had been called on to prepare for the Help a Little Club, an organization of ladies of Maria's church, who met weekly to sew for charity and to gossip. Always, hitherto, as he had carried the rugs into the back yard, he had cursed the club for that addition to his labors; and so he did on this occasion. But suddenly, as he was arranging the paper and kindling in the grate, he recognized opportunity. He stopped, stood up, and frowned.

"Great legs!" he cried; and repeated: "Great *legs!*"

And as he finished laying the fire, a continual grin of humorous and vengeful expectancy covered his face.

That afternoon he made his simple preparations. They consisted of a trip to the paint shop on Eighth Avenue, where he procured a ten-cent can of black paint and a small brush. He carried them to the cellar and concealed them in an old barrel.

Thursday morning came, and with it a display of un-exampled energy on the part of Mr. Chidden. The furnace ashes were attended to before breakfast, and by nine o'clock he had completed all the tasks that usually took him till noon. This was a mistake, but it was perceived by no one.

At twenty minutes past nine, Mr. Comicci came down the stairs and went into the street for his morning walk. Mr. Chidden witnessed his departure from the dining-room window. He waited five minutes, then went to the cellar for his paint and brush. As he came back up, he threw a hasty glance into the kitchen, where his sister Maria and Minnie were busied in the preparation of dain-ties for the expected guests. Then he passed swiftly up-stairs to the third floor and entered Mr. Comicci's room.

Straight to the table in the corner he went, and drew off the dark cloth. He had no time to be embarrassed by the nudity of the marble lady; he had work to do. He took his brush and paint and went at it. In ten minutes he had finished. He replaced the cloth, hid the brush and paint under his coat, and returned to the cellar, where he buried the implements under a pile of wood.

"There!" he breathed, his heart still thumping from a sensation of perilous adventure. "If only the dago don't lift that cloth! Well, it's a chance!"

There was nothing to do now but wait for afternoon and the arrival of the Help a Little Club. But the wait was not so tedious as it might have been, after Mr. Comicci had returned from his walk, for he spent most of the time loitering about the lower hall, expecting momentarily to hear a door thrown violently open upstairs and the voice of the Italian raised in wrath. But neither of these sounds came, though the guests did.

At the appearance of the first of them, a little after two o'clock, Mr. Chidden retreated to the floor above, having been instructed by Maria to keep out of the way. By three the parlor was full, and Mr. Chidden could hear the confused hum of their voices through the closed door. He could imagine them—old ladies, middle-aged ladies, fat ladies, lean ladies, amiable ladies, sour ladies, sitting in two or three circles, with both their tongues and needles running at the rate of two hundred strokes a second.

He had decided to wait till four o'clock before beginning operations, but half an hour before that time arrived, he was frightfully impatient; and he kept listening fearfully for indications of the discovery of his plot upstairs. At length he could bear it no longer. He made his way, with a strange reluctance, to the door of the third-floor front. There he hesitated, then raised his hand and knocked sharply. The Italian's voice came:

"Come in!"

As he opened the door, Mr. Chidden couldn't help sending a quick glance toward the rear corner, and he gave a little sigh of relief as he saw that the table and its cloth-covered statue were in their normal position. He turned to Mr. Comicci, who stood in an attitude of polite inquiry.

"My sister Maria sent me up," said he. "She's got some lady friends visiting, and she wants to know if she can bring them up to look at your things."

Of course, Mr. Comicci made no difficulty about it. He said it would make him very happy to show the ladies his poor things, only the room was very untidy——But that was to be expected of an artist.

"Sure," Mr. Chidden agreed. "They'll be right up."

He turned and went back downstairs. At the parlor door, he did not hesitate. Time was precious now. The Italian might begin to uncover things. His knock brought Maria herself to the door.

"What do you want?" she demanded impatiently, when she saw her brother.

"Mr. Comicci sent me," he replied, "to ask if you would

like to bring the ladies up to look at his things. I think he
expects he might sell something. Trashy stone!"

"Why, certainly," she replied, after a second's thought.
"Of course! It's very kind of him. Tell him we'll be up—
let's see—in half an hour."

Mr. Chidden was ready for this.

"He said," he continued calmly, "that he has to go out
right away, and would be obliged if you'd come at once."

"Well—I don't know——" Miss Maria hesitated; then
added: "All right. Tell him we'll be up right away."

Mr. Chidden remounted the stairs. His heart was
thumping violently.

"Subtle mashination," he breathed to himself. "Machi-
avelli. Italian work. I'll show the dago!"

He found Mr. Comicci trying to straighten up the room,
throwing pieces of clothing into the wardrobe, picking bits
of paper and clay from the floor, hiding the disreputable
grate with a still more disreputable square of drapery. Mr.
Chidden pitched in to help him. He brought a broom from
the closet in the hall and swept the floor, while the Italian
wiped off the chairs with a rag. Then together they arranged the objects for display on two boxes placed together in the middle of the room. There were dozens of
them—clay models, plaster casts, white and mongrel
marble, in all stages approaching completion. They had
not quite finished emptying the bottom drawer of the
wardrobe when they heard steps and voices on the stairs.

"They're coming!" whispered Mr. Chidden, throwing
the broom under the bed and retreating precipitately to a
corner—the one farthest away from the table with the
cloth-covered statue. The Italian threw on his coat, opened
the door, and stood bowing on the threshold as the ladies
approached, led by Miss Maria. He met her eyes with a
tender glance.

"This is so kind of you, Mr. Comicci!" said she melt-
ingly.

They entered. What a crew! Confusion! There was Mrs.

Rankin, gray, but aggressive, with quick, dark eyes that darted continually; Mrs. Manger, with humble air and sharp tongue; the three Misses Bipp, echoes of the past and of one another; Mrs. Paulton, who had once lived on Riverside Drive; Mrs. Judson, grandmotherly sweet; and a dozen others. Mr. Chidden watched them from his corner as they trooped in, jostling one another at the door, and standing foolishly still when they got in, just as they do in a street car. He wanted to cry: "Move forward; plenty of room in front!" but he was occupied principally with speculations of his own.

They grouped themselves around the two boxes, after a general introduction to Mr. Comicci, with little ejaculations of pleasure and foolish remarks. Mrs. Rankin asked if they might handle, and picked up a piece before Mr. Comicci had time to reply. The others followed suit. They carried the things nearer the windows, for a better light, and pointed out to one another the more subtle excellences. But Mr. Chidden chuckled to himself as he observed that certain figures—those without drapery— remained untouched and uncriticized.

"Now, this tiger!" said Mrs. Paulton. "Such beautiful lines!"

"It is very fine," agreed some one, "but the tail appears to be elongated."

They gathered around the tiger.

"It *is* a long tail," said Mrs. Rankin.

"Tigers have long tails," retorted Miss Maria in the tone of a champion.

"Still, this tail is so *very* long!"

"Quite too long, I should say."

"It *is* a long tail."

"For a tail, it *does* seem too long."

"A *little* too long," said Mrs. Paulton, with finality, and they passed to something else.

As time passed, and the fire of appreciation and criticism began to die down, Mr. Chidden began to get wor-

ried. Was it possible that Mr. Comicci did not intend to
show his masterpiece? It began to look that way. Mr.
Chidden made a resolution; he would wait five minutes,
then go and speak to one of the ladies about it. He began
to count the seconds.

He was saved by a little woman in light blue, one of
the younger ones, who had begun wandering about in search
of things. Her voice suddenly sounded above hubbub:

"Mr. Comicci! What is this? May I see?"

Mr. Chidden began to tremble as he saw that her hand
was on the dark cloth. Would it work?

The Italian, who was gesticulating excitedly in an effort
to explain the secrets of his art to Miss Maria and Mrs.
Judson, glanced across, with a look of uneasiness.

"Why—I don't know—" he said.

"You see—you might not like——"

"Why not?" demanded Mrs. Rankin.

"I don't know——" he stammered.

"But yes—why not? Of course. You may look. No!
Wait! Let me remove eet, signora. Eet verra easy fall."

The ladies gathered around the table in a close group
as the sculptor approached and laid his hands on the cloth.
They would seem to have foreseen in some mysterious
way what was to follow. From his corner, Mr. Chidden
watched them, and noted, with satisfaction, that Maria,
with Mrs. Rankin and the Misses Bipp, were together in
the front rank, up against the table.

"Eet is the true beauty," the Italian was saying. "The
line—the form—so pure and beautiful—nothing so beautiful——"

He removed the cloth.

After all, perhaps the good ladies saw only what they
expected to see, as far as the sculpture was concerned.
But the effect of nudity that came from that statue suddenly uncovered in their midst was startling. It was a
rather large figure, and so completely naked! So pro-
foundly naked! And it was well done! The marble white-

ness of body and limbs had a wonderful fleshlike appearance, so subtle were the lines, the little elevations and depressions, so skillfully and lovingly chiseled. They stood and looked at that statue of an exposed female form; and they saw on the rough marble at its foot, painted with black paint in small but precise capital letters:

MISS MARIA CHIDDEN.

A gasp of amazement and horror came from eighteen throats. They looked at Maria Chidden and back again at the statue, and they were dangerously near explosion from the supreme awfulness of the thing. It was an excellent instance of the lack of reason in the feminine mind. To any reasonable eye, even one totally unskilled in the perception of form, it must have been patently manifest that the proportions of the lady in marble were certainly not the proportions of Miss Maria Chidden; the thing could have been considered a representation of that attenuated dame only by an heroic application of the theory of idealization. But they did not think of that; they saw this reproduction of a female person without any clothes on, and they saw the label. Their faces turned all colors from ghostly pale to purple, and they stood speechless.

The horrified silence was broken by Miss Maria herself. "Wretch!" she screamed, and made a dive for Mr. Comicci.

The Italian, springing aside, barely missed her clutching fingers, and caused two of the Misses Bipp to sit down abruptly on the floor. He escaped by leaping over their prostrate forms. Then confusion and babel. As the Misses Bipp went down, the others screamed, and the more timid made for the door. The third Miss Bipp sank into a chair and began to moan. Miss Maria continued to clutch frantically, and shout "Wretch!" at the top of her voice, but the Italian kept our of reach behind the others, shouting back meanwhile:

"No, no, no, I did not do eet! No, no, no, signora!"

Mrs. Rankin and Mrs. Manger assisted the fallen Bipps to arise, and led them to the door; the others had by this time crowded into the hall. They hustled them out.

Miss Maria stood in the middle of the floor, trembling and choking with rage.

"No, no, no!" shouted the Italian, dancing up and down in front of her. "I did not do eet! See! Eet could not be—eet is small, plump; and you, you are—what you say?—you are skinny, beeg——"

"Wretch!" screamed Maria.

The Italian jumped back. Then he stopped suddenly and let out a fearful Italian oath. He glanced toward the corner where Mr. Chidden had last been seen. It was empty. The whole room was empty. Of Mr. Chidden there was neither sight nor sound, and from the hall came the chorus of the ladies' voices as they trooped downstairs.

"That—I did not do eet!" cried Mr. Comicci, trying to seize Maria's hand. "No, no, no! So pure and beautiful!"

She threw at him an awful look of concentrated scorn. She flew to the door.

"Miserable dago!" she said in a choking voice. The door slammed after her.

It was, on the whole, I think, a stroke of genius, for it must be remembered that Mr. Chidden appreciated the necessity for witnesses; also, that he secured the very best possible. It is true that it gave him a lot of extra work; he spent most of Saturday cleaning up the room, from which Mr. Comicci was ejected Friday morning. But his heart was light and his soul buoyant, and he sang as he worked. And it may as well be recorded that when he went to the movies on Eighth Avenue on Saturday evening, he wore a new pair of pants.

THE STRONG MAN

The poet was locked in his room and Mrs. Mannerlys, his hostess, had the key. Probably she had read somewhere of the method adopted by Lady Gregory to get work out of Yeats; but still Mrs. Mannerlys was capable of having thought it up for herself. Her cousin, the poet, was a lazy fellow who would not drive himself to work, so in the interests of literature she had taken him out to her country place and shut him up for four hours every day, first removing all books and placing fresh pens and paper on a table at the window.

. . . Where his muscles swelled.
And will and force and courage: ever dwelled.
Therein his strength; until he saw and heard her;
Then his heart trembled, and all his strength was weakness.

"Impossible," thought the poet disgustedly. "It sounds like Vers Libre. I'll have to take the line out. But it's exactly what I want to say: 'Then his heart trembled, and all his strength was weakness.' It'll have to be chopped

up, but 'weakness' must have a strong pause. It's enough
to drive you mad."

He threw his pen on the table and walked to the window, where he stood looking down into the garden and
on the long, sloping lawn with great shade trees and here
and there a clump of shrubbery or low laca bushes. Further away he could see the tennis court and the lake and
three or four figures of people moving about, one of them
in the act of launching a boat. He watched them a little
while without being conscious of what he saw, then his
gaze slowly traveled back toward the house. And then, in
the garden almost directly beneath his window, his eye
caught the light from a spot of blue in a hammock swung
beneath two trees. It was a woman's dress.

The eyes of the poet quickened, and he softly opened
the window and leaned across the sill, but the woman's
face remained hidden behind the end of the hammock.
The poet left the window and went to the door and turned
the knob.

"Oh, it's locked," he said stupidly, as though he had
not known it before. He raised his hand to knock on the
panel, then let it fall after a moment's hesitation and returned to the window. Stopping only for a glance at the
spot of blue in the hammock, he clambered onto the sill
and swung himself out, catching the farther edge of the
shutter. There he hung for a moment, twenty feet above
the ground, then with a quick, agile movement he threw
his body sharply to one side and wrapped his legs and
arms around a drainpipe five feet away, while the shutter
banged against the side of the house with a loud noise
and a cry of surprise and alarm came from below. The
poet slid easily down the drain pipe to the ground and
began dusting off his clothes.

"Good heavens!" came a voice from the hammock.
"It's a wonder you didn't kill yourself!"

The poet looked up quickly with an expression of the
keenest disappointment. What he saw was a young

woman of twenty-three or four with rather ordinary brown hair, a clear, high brow. fine dark eyes and a full pleasant face divided in the middle by a delicately thin nose. Not a displeasing sight, surely; but the poet's tone was certainly one of displeasure as he took a step forward and observed:

"Oh, it's you. Where did you get that dress?"

"Why, I—well, I'm not surprised. I've often said you're crazy."

"What right have you got to wear that dress?"

"*Well*! It's 'a poor thing, but mine own.' It came from Herbert, on Fifth Avenue, if you must know. And now, my dear Paul, perhaps you'll explain why you've taken to climbing through windows to slide down drainpipes and ask your lady friends where they buy their clothes."

The poet grunted, seated himself on the grass beside the hammock and hugged his knees.

"It deceived me," he said dismally.

"I thought it was someone else. Dress exactly the same. And I wanted to speak to her, and Helen had me locked in the room, so I came that way. It was all for nothing, and now I can't get back. Got a cigarette?"

"It's Kitty Vreeland," said the young woman with a laugh. "But where is your poet's observation? See these stripes? Kitty hasn't any. And the cut is entirely different."

"I can't help it; I'm not a costume designer. Anyway, I couldn't see from the window. What day is today?"

"Friday."

"Is she coming? Helen wouldn't tell me."

"No. She's spending a week at Newport." The young woman added maliciously, "And I believe Massitot is there, too."

"I don't care," replied the poet indifferently, "as long as she's not here. I just wanted to look at her. Who's coming?"

"I don't know—Helen's usual crowd."

"Wortley, Townsend, Crevel?"

"I suppose so."

"And Richard the Great?"

"I really don't know. Oh, it would be absurd to pretend not to know who you mean. Only it's ridiculous."

"Of course." The poet looked up amusedly at the little frown on her brow, then smiled softly to himself. "Of course it's ridiculous. Really he's no greater than any of the others, only he thinks he is, and it's the same thing. You see, Janet, you must look at it as he does. At twenty-seven he set out to do a certain thing, and at the end of six years he is nearer his goal than most men can get in a lifetime. He has made lots of money, and he has developed a power. He is a strong man, measured by the requirements of the modern arena. What if he is conceited in his strength? So is every man who has any. So am I."

"But why do you say all this to me?"

"Because you ought to hear it. I see things. I am a poet. I won't be one much longer, because I'm beginning to get clever, and that is fatal. It's my accursed laziness. I was composing today, and I had Richard Gorrin in mind.

. . . until he saw and heard her,
Then his heart trembled, and all his strength was weakness.' "

"Good heavens! Not Richard the Great!"

"Certainly."

"But that's impossible!"

"By no means."

"You don't know him, my dear Paul."

The sudden note of bitterness in her tone caused him to look up at her, and his glance was so quick and unexpected that he caught the smile, equally bitter, on her lips, before she had time to erase it. He looked away again, and his expression of amusement gave way to one of thoughtfulness.

"You don't understand," he said, presently. "I don't mean that his strength turns into weakness. The contrary. When his heart trembles with love his weakness is his real strength. It's a good thing we're such old friends, Janet. No man likes to explain his verses."

"Especially when they're absurd."

"Absurd!"

"I mean, in this particular instance. You don't know Mr. Gorrin. He is all strength. He has no weakness."

Again the bitter note; and something else—was it wistfulness, regret, sorrow? Not exactly, perhaps, but something very like it.

"Of course!" cried the poet, leaping to his feet. "Of course! That's it! I should have seen it before! The trouble is, Janet, you're too intellectual. You need a grain more of womanish intuition. No, don't pretend with me. Don't you think I see things? Don't you think I know when a woman's in love? Only I couldn't understand—"

"Paul—please——"

"No, no, no! And you think Richard Gorrin is all strength. How funny! I can see him now; I can hear him, with his offers to protect and cherish. How funny! There's a great deal too much strength about, Janet. You're as bad as he is. I really think I must change that line to something more comprehensive."

"Paul, I am positively going in unless——"

"No, you're not. Wait a minute, I want to think. One thing, of course, would be very simple—I don't know— I may try it—yet, I will! It will be very funny, and it will prove I'm right. It's a good thing we're old friends, Janet; you won't mind my experimenting."

The poet paused to brush back his hair into a semblance of order, approached the hammock so that he stood directly in front of her, and bowed formally.

"Miss Beaton," he said, "will you marry me?"

"Well! Really——"

"No, you must answer 'yes.' Of course you don't want to, but neither do I, and I'll break it off tomorrow. A poet never keeps a promise anyway, and I'm not in love with you, so you may know I shan't hold you to it. Will you marry me? Say yes. It's an experiment. Will you marry me?"

The lady's lips were parted in an amused smile.

"Yes, my dear poet," she said.

"You will?"

"Yes."

"Good!" He took her hand and kissed the fingers. "Then that's understood. We're engaged. You'll see I'm right. And now, of course, you want to be left alone to think; they always do. As for me, I've got two hours till dinner to repair that infernal line, and in forty minutes the train arrives with Richard the Great and the rest of them. I will retire with my newfound happiness; and by the way, Janet, next time you camp out under my window wear a different dress. It's confusing."

And so he left her.

Four hours later Miss Janet Beaton was back again in the hammock. It was night now, and all you could see of the shade trees was a great mass of dark blotches against the starlight in the sky, save where a shaft of yellow rays fell here and there from a window of the house. It was a cool, fresh evening in early June, and Miss Beaton had wrapped a mantle about her shoulders to keep off the dew.

Around a corner of the house, from a distance, sounded the faint cries and bursts of laughter of those who were playing tennis under the electric lights on the courts; others of the weekend guests had taken boats on the lake. Miss Beaton had managed with some difficulty to separate herself from the crowd, and had sought refuge here to think. She lay back in the hammock looking up at a lighted window—the same window through which the poet had clambered that afternoon, and behind which he was sitting now, tinkering with words.

"It was very silly," mused the lady in an undertone. "I had no idea he meant to tell everyone. And if he really thought that Richard Gorrin could be jealous—but how childish! He didn't mean that at all. Anyway, it was amusing to see their faces——"

She stopped and raised her head quickly, then as quickly dropped it again. Someone had suddenly appeared around the corner of the house, a dim form in the semi-darkness, calling her name.

"Miss Beaton! I say, Miss Beaton!"

Janet lay silent. The figure advanced and stopped in the path of light from a window. It was that of a tall, vigorous-looking man, not much over thirty, with a strong, expressive, agreeable face and straight, determined carriage.

"Miss Beaton!" he repeated, moving forward.

She saw that he was coming toward the hammock, so she sat up and said calmly:

"Well. Here I am."

He approached and stood above her.

"Ah! I thought you were coming to the lake. You said——"

"I changed my mind."

"But couldn't you have told us——"

"I called, but you were too far ahead."

He did not reply, but walked to a nearby tree for a garden stool, which he brought back and placed beside the hammock. Then he seated himself and lit a cigar.

"I don't want to keep you away," said Janet presently.

"Away from what?"

"The lake—the others."

He grunted, puffing his cigar. There was silence for several minutes, during which Janet leaned back in the hammock giving thanks that it was too dark for him to see her face plainly; it is easier to talk when you do not have to control your expression and your voice at the same time. Suddenly Gorrin rose to his feet and threw the cigar on the ground with an impatient gesture.

"Look here," he said abruptly, "what is this nonsense about you and Duval?"

Janet, looking up at the lighted window behind which
the poet sat, smiled to herself, and her heart was filled
with gratitude toward him. He had been wrong, but he
had given her dignity—and yes, there could be no doubt
that he had foreseen this very question. It was the question
of a strong man, of a man who wins by strength. As for
the reply——

"Nonsense?" she repeated, in a tone of polite inquiry.

"Yes. Of course it's nonsense. You don't expect me to
believe you really intend to marry him?"

"Why not?"

"For several reasons. One is, he's a dreamer, a dallier;
you're too intelligent. Another, you are going to marry
me."

Janet raised herself to lean on her elbow.

"Now you are talking nonsense," she said quietly.

"No, I'm merely repeating the truth. You've heard it
before."

Gorrin took a step nearer the hammock.

"Look here, Janet, you're a sensible woman, why play
with serious questions? Why will you try to postpone the
inevitable? Answer this: did you tell me once, not a year
ago, that you loved me?"

"Oh," said Janet impatiently, "are you going to begin
that again?"

"Yes, I'm going to begin that. You did tell me you
loved me. Why? You say, because you thought you did.
But you're intelligent; you don't make such an admission
lightly. You must have loved me. And I loved you. I love
you now. But you won't promise to marry me. I ask you
why? You say I don't really love you. You say I am too
strong to need you, therefore I can know nothing of love."

"No, I said——"

"Pardon me. It would be idle to deny my strength. I
use it every day, in everything I do. I am a strong man;
that's why I can't fall before you on my knees like a poet
and talk sweet. It isn't in me. And as I have told you

many times, with that strength I am going to win you. Don't mistake me. It was not jealousy that brought me here to ask you about that fool Duval. But accidents may happen to anyone, and I wish to guard against them. That is why I want to know what this nonsense means. Why did Duval tell us tonight that you have promised to marry him? It's absurd, anyway. It is not done that way."

Janet was thinking. She was asking herself: after all, are these words dictated by strength? And she felt the answer in her heart; it trembled within her. How blind she had been! She was doubly glad now that her face could not be seen clearly, for her eyes were moist. She felt ashamed of herself, of her womanliness, or lack of it, not to have known before. Only she must make sure. No mistakes now. So, summoning all her courage and cunning, she made her tone light, almost impersonal, as she said:

"But you forget that Paul is a poet. He does everything differently."

"Bah! What is it—a wager?"

"A little more——" Janet raised herself, "a little more, and you will offend me. Really. I mean that, Mr. Gorrin."

He looked up quickly at the new seriousness in her tone.

"But what am I to believe? I do not mean to offend. You and Duval have been—you are like brother and sister. You know him too well. It's absurd. You would never marry so useless, so incapable——"

"Mr. Gorrin!"

He stopped.

"This afternoon," said Janet quietly, "I promised to marry Paul Duval."

"I know, but——"

"That is all."

"You promised to marry him?"

"Yes."

He straightened up, and it was with an entirely new voice that he said:

"Janet, you're not really serious?"

She stirred and moved her head to look at him.

"What a pity," she said, "that you will continue to delude yourself."

"Delude myself? I am not in the habit——"

"Yes, you are. You are, Mr. Gorrin. After all, I can't expect you to believe unless I explain. Yes, a year ago I said I loved you. No matter why—I don't know. Then I saw I had been mistaken. I began to know you, better than you know yourself. You have asked me many times to marry you. Why?"

"Because I love you."

"Very well, but why?"

"Why—of course—to have you, to protect and cherish you, to defend you——"

"Defend me from what?"

"From the world."

"Well, you see, that's just it; I don't want anyone to defend me from the world. But the real reason is that you're spoiled. You want me as a child wants a cookie. That's where your strength deceives and betrays you, and where it will fail you. Some day you will really fall in love, and then see what your strength amounts to. As for me, I am engaged to Paul—and you regard it as a joke. That is why I am trying to explain to you, so you won't annoy me any more."

"Annoy you! Janet——"

"Yes, annoy me. You have done so for months. Your belief in yourself has been so certain! So pitiful. So childlike and Byronesque. For a time it was amusing; it has become a nuisance. And now that I am engaged to Paul it must end. He is up there in his room now. Shall I call him down to satisfy you?"

She stopped, expecting an outburst. These were strong words for a Richard Gorrin to swallow. But he was silent. She could not see his face plainly in the darkness, but she was aware somehow of its tenseness, of its expression of white astonishment. No, he would not show his rage; he was too strong for that. She found herself wondering how she had happened to hit on the word "Byronesque"; how keenly it would cut him! Yes, no doubt he would turn and go without a word. She shivered. What horrible thing was this she was doing to herself? Paul had been wrong, wrong, wrong!

Suddenly Gorrin spoke.

"You are making a mistake, Janet——"

A curious thing happened. He had begun in almost his usual tones, firm, sure, decided; but as he pronounced her name an odd sound came from his throat, as though he had suddenly choked, and he stopped. A little quiver ran up from Janet's heart, and she thought to herself, "If I could only see his face, I would know!"

"I have had no thought of offending you," said Gorrin, finding his voice again. "It hurts me to have you say that. I have honestly thought all the time that you were in love with me, and I——"

"And so you bullied me," she interrupted.

"I am sorry you think me capable of that."

"It's true. You bullied me. I admit I deliberately led you on, because I thought you needed the lesson. And—it amused me. But now—now that Paul and I—it must stop. Take your strength somewhere else, Mr. Gorrin."

"Janet, I love you."

She trembled from head to foot. He had never said it like that before. But that was not enough.

"Mr. Gorrin," she said, "you are talking to an engaged woman."

Then she bit her lip. How silly to have used that conventionally heroic phrase! But he did not notice.

"I can't help it. I love you."

"No—I must not listen——"

"You will listen! No, I don't mean that—I only mean I can't believe—yes—you *must* listen! Do you think I'm going to let you go? You accuse me of feeling secure in

my strength! I do! As for *him*, I don't give that for him.
Nor for anyone else. You're mine. Yes, you see now,
Janet, what it means to me. It is simply that I must have
you, and he—he is not to be thought of—he——"

He stopped. Janet had suddenly twisted herself about
in the hammock so that she faced the lighted window
above, and called in a clear, loud voice:

"Paul!"

Gorrin turned instinctively. Almost at once the shade
flew up, then the window was opened, and the poet leaned
out with his hands on the sill, peering into the darkness.

"Paul, are you busy?"

"What—who—oh, Janet? Why—yes—no."

"I'm coming up."

"All right. I dare you."

Janet slipped out of the hammock to the ground as the
window was closed above.

"You see, Mr. Gorrin, I *won't* listen——" she began,
then stopped short with astonishment at sight of his face.
It was pale with stupefaction and amazement, but it was
drawn and tight, too, like that of a man who has suddenly
encountered some unexpected and overwhelming catastrophe and is using all his strength to keep from crying out
in misery.

"My God," he murmured, "you actually meant it—you
mean to——Janet——"

She could not bear it a moment longer, so without a
word she went swiftly past him to the walk and around
that to the door of the house. At the corner she turned,
but she could not see him near the hammock. Then she
entered the hall and ran swiftly up the stairs and down
the corridor, and knocked on a door at the end. It was
opened immediately.

As soon as the poet saw her face he whistled expres-
sively, and a smile appeared on his lips.

"Ah," he said, "I take it you were not alone down there.
I thought I discerned a dim and massive form on the

greensward." He stepped aside to allow her to pass. "Come in."

"No," she replied hurriedly, "I can't. I just wanted—he is down there. Oh Paul, you were right! I was a silly girl. I guess I'm talking like one. I'm going—but wait—first, we're not really engaged, you know. That is—what am I saying?—I don't want to be."

"What!" exclaimed the poet reproachfully. "You want to break our engagement!"

"Yes. That is—we never *were* engaged—I just wanted——"

"Indeed! Janet, you wound me. You even break my heart. You ruin my life. It was distinctly understood——"

"Silly!" cried Janet.

She stepped forward, raised herself and kissed him.

"There!" she cried, and turned and left him.

She went back down the stairs even faster than she had come up. But in the lower hall she slackened her pace, and when she reached the porch she came to a stop; and she felt a warm flush pass over her whole body so that the roots of her hair tingled. She stood still for a moment, then moved forward again, but slowly and as if reluctantly. She found herself again on the path that led to the garden; then the thought came, "What if he is not there?" and her step quickened. She turned the corner of the house, straining her eyes——No, she could not see him.

Still she went forward, and it seemed to her that her feet made a frightful commotion on the gravel. She was quite close now, and was just thinking that he had certainly gone, when a curious noise reached her ears, like the sound of someone choking or snoring, but not quite that. It was an odd, unprecedented noise. Then she saw that there was something in the hammock. Her heart pounded in her breast. She approached on tiptoe and saw him lying there, face down, his shoulders shaking convulsively and strange sounds coming from his throat.

Richard the Great was crying.

Her heart stopped beating, and it seemed to swell in her bosom and fill her with an overpowering, delicious warmth as she stooped down and placed her cheek against his and murmured his name.